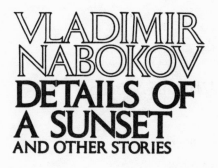

VLADIMIR
NABOKOV
DETAILS OF
A SUNSET
AND OTHER STORIES

Books by Vladimir Nabokov

Ada, a novel

Bend Sinister, a novel

The Defense, a novel

Despair, a novel

Details of a Sunset and Other Stories

Eugene Onegin, by Alexander Pushkin,
    translated from the Russian, with a Commentary

The Eye, a novel

The Gift, a novel

Glory, a novel

Invitation to a Beheading, a novel

King, Queen, Knave, a novel

Laughter in the Dark, a novel

Lolita, a novel

Lolita: A Screenplay

Look at the Harlequins!, a novel

Mary, a novel

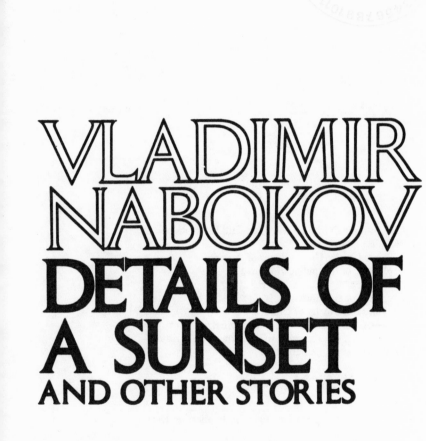

VLADIMIR NABOKOV
DETAILS OF A SUNSET
AND OTHER STORIES

McGraw-Hill Book Company
New York • St. Louis • San Francisco • Toronto

123456789BPBP79876

Library of Congress Cataloging in Publication Data

Nabokov, Vladimir Vladimirovich, 1899–
    Details of a sunset and other stories.

    CONTENTS: Details of a sunset.—A bad day.—Orache.
—The return of Chorb. [etc.]
    I. Title.
PZ3.N121Dg [PG3476.N3]   891.7'3'42   75-34086
ISBN 0-07-045709-3

The following stories appeared originally in *The New Yorker*: "Christmas," "A Guide to Berlin," and "A Slice of Life." "The Doorbell" originally appeared in *Playboy*.

To Véra

CONTENTS

Foreword

This collection is the last batch of my Russian stories meriting to be Englished. They cover a period of eleven years (1924–1935); all of them appeared in the émigré dailies and magazines of the time, in Berlin, Riga, and Paris.

It may be helpful, in some remote way, if I give here a list of all my translated stories, as published, in four separate volumes in the U.S.A. during the last twenty years.

Nabokov's Dozen (New York, Doubleday, 1958) includes the following three stories translated by Peter Pertzov in collaboration with the author:

1. "Spring in Fialta" (Vesna v Fial'te, 1936)
2. "The Aurelian" (Pil'gram, 1930)
3. "Cloud, Castle, Lake" (Oblako, ozero, bashnya, 1937)

A Russian Beauty (New York, McGraw-Hill, 1973) contains the following thirteen stories translated by Dmitri Nabokov in collaboration with the author, except for the title story translated by Simon Karlinsky in collaboration with the author:

4. "A Russian Beauty" (Krasavitsa, 1934)
5. "The Leonardo" (Korolyok, 1933)
6. "Torpid Smoke" (Tyazhyolyy dym, 1935)
7. "Breaking the News" (Opoveshchenie, 1935)
8. "Lips to Lips" (Usta k ustam, 1932)
9. "The Visit to the Museum" (Poseshchenie muzeya, 1931)
10. "An Affair of Honor" (Podlets, 1927)
11. "Terra Incognita" (same title, 1931)
12. "A Dashing Fellow" (Khvat, 1930)
13. "Ultima Thule" (same title, 1940)
14. "Solus Rex" (same title, 1940)
15. "The Potato Elf" (Kartofel'nyy el'f, 1929)
16. "The Circle" (Krug, 1934)

Tyrants Destroyed (New York, McGraw-Hill, 1975) includes twelve stories translated by Dmitri Nabokov in collaboration with the author:

17. "Tyrants Destroyed" (Istreblenie tiranov, 1938)
18. "A Nursery Tale" (Skazka, 1926)
19. "Music" (Muzyka, 1932)
20. "Lik" (same title, 1939)
21. "Recruiting" (Nabor, 1935)
22. "Terror" (Uzhas, 1927)
23. "The Admiralty Spire" (Admiralteyskaya igla, 1933)
24. "A Matter of Chance" (Sluchaynost', 1924)
25. "In Memory of L. I. Shigaev" (Pamyati L. I. Shigaeva, 1934)
26. "Bachman" (same title, 1924)

27. "Perfection" (Sovershenstvo, 1932)
28. "Vasiliy Shishkov" (same title, 1939)

Details of a Sunset (New York, McGraw-Hill, 1976) contains thirteen stories translated by Dmitri Nabokov in collaboration with the author:

29. "Details of a Sunset" (Katastrofa, 1924)
30. "A Bad Day" (Obida, 1931)
31. "Orache" (Lebeda, 1932)
32. "The Return of Chorb" (Vozvrashchenie Chorba, 1925)
33. "The Passenger" (Passazhir, 1927)
34. "A Letter that Never Reached Russia" (Pis'mo v Rossiyu, 1925)
35. "A Guide to Berlin" (Putevoditel' po Berlinu, 1925)
36. "The Doorbell" (Zvonok, 1927)
37. "The Thunderstorm" (Groza, 1924)
38. "The Reunion" (Vstrecha, 1932)
39. "A Slice of Life" (Sluchay iz zhizni, 1935)
40. "Christmas" (Rozhdestvo, 1925)
41. "A Busy Man" (Zanyatoy chelovek, 1931)

Vladimir Nabokov
Montreux, 1975

DETAILS OF A SUNSET

I doubt very much that I was responsible for the odious title ("Katastrofa") inflicted upon this story. It was written in June 1924 in Berlin and sold to the Riga émigré daily Segodnya where it appeared on July 13 of that year. Still under that label, and no doubt with my indolent blessings, it was included in the collection Soglyadatay, Slovo, *Berlin, 1930.*

I have now given it a new title, one that has the triple advantage of corresponding to the thematic background of the story, of being sure to puzzle such readers as "skip descriptions," and of infuriating reviewers.

The last streetcar was disappearing in the mirrorlike murk of the street and, along the wire above it, a spark of Bengal light, crackling and quivering, sped into the distance like a blue star.

"Well, might as well just plod along, even though you are pretty drunk, Mark, pretty drunk. . . ."

The spark went out. The roofs glistened in the moonlight, silvery angles broken by oblique black cracks.

Through this mirrory darkness he staggered home: Mark Standfuss, a salesclerk, a demigod, fair-haired Mark, a lucky fellow with a high starched collar. At the back of his neck, above the white line of that collar, his hair ended in a funny, boyish little tag that had escaped the barber's scissors. That little tag was what made Klara fall in love with him, and she swore that it was true love, that she had quite forgotten the handsome ruined foreigner who last year had rented a room from her mother, Frau Heise.

"And yet, Mark, you're drunk. . . ."

That evening there had been beer and songs with friends in honor of Mark and russet-haired, pale Klara, and in a week they would be married; then there would be a lifetime of bliss and peace, and of nights with her, the red blaze of her hair spreading all over the pillow, and, in the morning, again her quiet laughter, the green dress, the coolness of her bare arms.

In the middle of a square stood a black wigwam: the tram tracks were being repaired. He remembered how today he had got under her short sleeve, and kissed the touching scar from her smallpox vaccination. And now he was walking home, unsteady on his feet from too much happiness and too much drink, swinging his slender cane, and among the dark houses on the opposite side of the empty street a night echo clop-clopped in time with his footfalls; but grew silent when he turned at the corner where the same man as always, in apron and peaked cap, stood by his grill, selling frankfurters, crying out in a tender and sad birdlike whistle: "*Würstchen, würstchen. . . .*"

Mark felt a sort of delicious pity for the frankfurters, the moon, the blue spark that had receded along the wire, and, as he tensed his body against a friendly fence, he was overcome with laughter, and, bending, exhaled into a little round hole in the boards the words "Klara, Klara, oh my darling!"

On the other side of the fence, in a gap between the buildings, was a rectangular vacant lot. Several moving vans stood there like enormous coffins. They were bloated from their loads. Heaven knows what was piled inside them. Oakwood trunks, probably, and chandeliers like iron spiders, and the heavy skeleton of a double bed. The moon cast a hard glare on the vans. To the left of the lot, huge black hearts were flattened against a bare rear wall—the shadows, many times magnified, of the leaves of a linden tree that stood next to a streetlamp on the edge of the sidewalk.

Mark was still chuckling as he climbed the dark stairs to his floor. He reached the final step, but mistakenly raised his foot again, and it came down awkwardly with a bang. While he was groping in the dark in search of the keyhole, his bamboo cane slipped out from under his arm and, with a subdued little clatter, slid down the staircase. Mark held his breath. He thought the cane would turn with the stairs and knock its way down to the bottom. But the high-pitched wooden click abruptly ceased. Must have stopped. He grinned with relief and, holding on to the banister (the beer singing in his hollow head), started to descend again. He nearly fell, and sat down heavily on a step, as he groped around with his hands.

Upstairs the door onto the landing opened. Frau Stand-fuss, with a kerosene lamp in her hand, half-dressed, eyes blinking, the haze of her hair showing from beneath her nightcap, came out and called, "Is that you, Mark?"

A yellow wedge of light encompassed the banisters, the stairs, and his cane, and Mark, panting and pleased, climbed up again to the landing, and his black, hunchbacked shadow followed him up along the wall.

Then, in the dimly lit room, divided by a red screen, the following conversation took place:

"You've had too much to drink, Mark."

"No, no, Mother ... I'm so happy ..."

"You've got yourself all dirty, Mark. Your hand is black...."

"... so very happy.... Ah, that feels good ... water's nice and cold. Pour some on the top of my head ... more.... Everybody congratulated me, and with good reason.... Pour some more on."

"But they say she was in love with somebody else such a short time ago—a foreign adventurer of some kind. Left without paying five marks he owed Frau Heise...."

"Oh, stop—you don't understand anything.... We did

such a lot of singing today . . . Look, I've lost a button. . . .
I think they'll double my salary when I get married. . . ."

"Come on, go to bed. . . . You're all dirty, and your new
pants, too."

That night Mark had an unpleasant dream. He saw his
late father. His father came up to him, with an odd smile
on his pale, sweaty face, seized Mark under the arms, and
began to tickle him silently, violently, and relentlessly.

He only remembered that dream after he had arrived at
the store where he worked, and he remembered it because
a friend of his, jolly Adolf, poked him in the ribs. For one
instant something flew open in his soul, momentarily froze
still in surprise, and slammed shut. Then again everything
became easy and limpid, and the neckties he offered his
customers smiled brightly, in sympathy with his happiness.
He knew he would see Klara that evening—he would only
run home for dinner, then go straight to her house. . . . The
other day, when he was telling her how cozily and tenderly
they would live, she had suddenly burst into tears. Of course
Mark had understood that these were tears of joy (as she
herself explained); she began whirling about the room, her
skirt like a green sail, and then she started rapidly smooth-
ing her glossy hair, the color of apricot jam, in front of the
mirror. And her face was pale and bewildered, also from
happiness, of course. It was all so natural, after all. . . .

"A striped one? Why certainly."

He knotted the tie on his hand, and turned it this way
and that, enticing the customer. Nimbly he opened the flat
cardboard boxes . . .

Meanwhile his mother had a visitor: Frau Heise. She had
come without warning, and her face was tear-stained.
Gingerly, almost as if she were afraid of breaking into

pieces, she lowered herself onto a stool in the tiny, spotless kitchen where Frau Standfuss was washing the dishes. A two-dimensional wooden pig hung on the wall, and a half-open matchbox with one burnt match lay on the stove.

"I have come to you with bad news, Frau Standfuss."

The other woman froze, clutching a plate to her chest.

"It's about Klara. Yes. She has lost her senses. That lodger of mine came back today—you know, the one I told you about. And Klara has gone mad. Yes, it all happened this morning. . . . She never wants to see your son again. . . . You gave her the material for a new dress; it will be returned to you. And here is a letter for Mark. Klara's gone mad. I don't know what to think. . . ."

Meanwhile Mark had finished work and was already on his way home. Crew-cut Adolf walked him all the way to his house. They both stopped, shook hands, and Mark gave a shove with his shoulder to the door which opened into cool emptiness.

"Why go home? The heck with it. Let's have a bite somewhere, you and I."

Adolf stood, propping himself on his cane as if it were a tail.

"The heck with it, Mark. . . ."

Mark gave his cheek an irresolute rub, then laughed.

"All right. Only it's my treat."

When, half an hour later, he came out of the pub and said good-bye to his friend, the flush of a fiery sunset filled the vista of the canal, and a rain-streaked bridge in the distance was margined by a narrow rim of gold along which passed tiny black figures.

He glanced at his watch and decided to go straight to his fiancée's without stopping at his mother's. His happiness and the limpidity of the evening air made his head spin a little. An arrow of bright copper struck the lacquered shoe of a fop jumping out of a car. The puddles, which still had not dried, surrounded by the bruise of dark damp (the live eyes of the asphalt), reflected the soft incandescence of the evening. The houses were as gray as ever; yet the roofs, the moldings above the upper floors, the gilt-edged lightning rods, the stone cupolas, the colonnettes—which nobody notices during the day, for day-people seldom look up— were now bathed in rich ochre, the sunset's airy warmth, and thus they seemed unexpected and magical, those upper protrusions, balconies, cornices, pillars, contrasting sharply, because of their tawny brilliance, with the drab façades beneath.

"Oh, how happy I am," Mark kept musing, "how everything around celebrates my happiness."

As he sat in the tram he tenderly, lovingly examined his fellow passengers. He had such a young face, had Mark, with pink pimples on the chin, glad luminous eyes, an untrimmed tag at the hollow of his nape.... One would think fate might have spared him.

"In a few moments I'll see Klara," he thought. "She'll meet me at the door. She'll say she barely survived until evening."

He gave a start. He had missed the stop where he should have got off. On the way to the exit he tripped over the feet of a fat gentleman who was reading a medical journal; Mark wanted to tip his hat but nearly fell: the streetcar was turning with a screech. He grabbed an overhead strap and managed to keep his balance. The man slowly retracted his short legs with a phlegmy and cross growl. He had a gray mustache which twisted up pugnaciously. Mark gave him a guilty smile and reached the front end of the car. He grasped the iron handrails with both hands, leaned forward, calculated his jump. Down below, the asphalt streamed past, smooth and glistening. Mark jumped. There was a burn of friction against his soles, and his legs started running by themselves, his feet stamping with involuntary resonance. Several odd things occurred simultaneously: from the front of the car, as it swayed away from Mark, the conductor emitted a furious shout; the shiny asphalt swept upward like the seat of a swing; a roaring mass hit Mark from behind. He felt as if a thick thunderbolt had gone through him from head to toe, and then nothing. He was standing alone on the glossy asphalt. He looked around. He saw, at a distance, his own figure, the slender back of Mark Standfuss, who was walking diagonally across the street as if nothing had happened. Marveling, he caught up with himself in one easy sweep, and now it was he nearing the sidewalk, his entire frame filled with a gradually diminishing vibration.

"That was stupid. Almost got run over by a bus...."

The street was wide and gay. The colors of the sunset had invaded half of the sky. Upper stories and roofs were bathed in glorious light. Up there, Mark could discern translucent porticoes, friezes and frescoes, trellises covered with orange roses, winged statues that lifted skyward golden, unbearably blazing lyres. In bright undulations, ethereally, festively, these architectonic enchantments were receding into the heavenly distance, and Mark could not understand how he had never noticed before those galleries, those temples suspended on high.

He banged his knee painfully. That black fence again. He could not help laughing as he recognized the vans beyond. There they stood, like gigantic coffins. Whatever might they conceal within? Treasures? The skeletons of giants? Or dusty mountains of sumptuous furniture?

"Oh, I must have a look. Or else Klara will ask, and I shan't know."

He gave a quick nudge to the door of one of the vans and went inside. Empty. Empty, except for one little straw chair in the center, comically poised askew on three legs.

Mark shrugged and went out on the opposite side. Once again the hot evening glow gushed into sight. And now in front of him was the familiar wrought-iron wicket, and further on Klara's window, crossed by a green branch. Klara herself opened the gate, and stood waiting, lifting her bared elbows, adjusting her hair. The russet tufts of her armpits showed through the sunlit openings of her short sleeves.

Mark, laughing noiselessly, ran up to embrace her. He pressed his cheek against the warm, green silk of her dress.

Her hands came to rest on his head.

"I was so lonely all day, Mark. But now you are here."

She opened the door, and Mark immediately found himself in the dining room, which struck him as being inordinately spacious and bright.

"When people are as happy as we are now," she said, "they can do without a hallway," Klara spoke in a passionate whisper, and he felt that her words had some special, wonderful meaning.

And in the dining room, around the snow-white oval of the tablecloth, sat a number of people, none of whom Mark had seen before at his fiancée's house. Among them was Adolf, swarthy, with his square-shaped head; there was also that short-legged, big-bellied old man who had been reading a medical journal in the tram and was still grumbling.

[24]

Mark greeted the company with a shy nod and sat down beside Klara, and in that same instant felt, as he had a short time ago, a bolt of atrocious pain pass through his whole frame. He writhed, and Klara's green dress floated away, diminished, and turned into the green shade of a lamp. The lamp was swaying on its cord. Mark was lying beneath it, with that inconceivable pain crushing his body, and nothing could be distinguished save that oscillating lamp, and his ribs were pressing against his heart, making it impossible to breathe, and someone was bending his leg, straining to break it, in a moment it would crack. He freed himself somehow, the lamp glowed green again, and Mark saw himself sitting a little way off, beside Klara, and no sooner had he seen it than he found himself brushing his knee against her warm silk skirt. And Klara was laughing, her head thrown back.

He felt an urge to tell about what had just happened, and, addressing all those present—jolly Adolf, the irritable fat man—uttered with an effort:

"The foreigner is offering the aforementioned prayers on the river. . . ."

It seemed to him that he had made everything clear, and apparently they had all understood. . . . Klara, with a little pout, pinched his cheek:

"My poor darling. It'll be all right. . . ."

He began to feel tired and sleepy. He put his arm around Klara's neck, drew her to him, and lay back. And then the pain pounced upon him again, and everything became clear.

Mark was lying supine, mutilated and bandaged, and the lamp was not swinging any longer. The familiar fat man with the mustache, now a doctor in a white gown, made worried growling small noises as he peered into the pupils of Mark's eyes. And what pain! . . . God, in a moment his heart would be impaled on a rib and burst . . . , God, any instant now. . . . This is silly. Why isn't Klara here. . . .

The doctor frowned and clucked his tongue.

Mark no longer breathed, Mark had departed—whither, into what other dreams, none can tell.

A BAD DAY

A Bad Day (*entitled in Russian* Obida, *the lexical meaning of which is "offense," "mortification," etc.*) *was written in Berlin in the summer of 1931. It appeared in the émigré daily* Poslednie Novosti (*Paris, July 12, 1931*) *and was included in my collection* Soglyadatay (*Paris, 1938*), *with a dedication to Ivan Bunin. The little boy of the story, though living in much the same surroundings as those of my own childhood, differs in several ways from my remembered self which is really split here among three lads, Peter, Vladimir, and Vasiliy.*

Peter sat on the box of the open carriage, next to the coachman (he was not particularly fond of that seat, but the coachman and everybody at home thought he liked it extremely, and he on his part did not want to hurt people, so this is how he came to be sitting there, a sallow-faced, gray-eyed youngster in a smart sailor blouse). The pair of well-fed black horses, with a gloss on their fat croups and something extraordinarily feminine about their long manes, kept lashing their tails in sumptuous fashion as they progressed at a rippling trot, and it pained one to observe how avidly, despite that movement of tails and that twitching of tender ears—despite, too, the thick tarry odor of the repellent in use—dull gray deerflies, or some big gadfly with shimmery eyes bulging, would stick to the sleek coats.

Coachman Stepan, a taciturn elderly man wearing a sleeveless vest of black velvet over a crimson Russian shirt, had a dyed beard and a brown neck lined with thin cracks. Peter felt embarrassed to keep silent while sitting on the same box; therefore he fixed his gaze on the middle shaft, on the traces, trying to invent a keen question or a sound remark. From time to time this or that horse would half-raise its tail, under the tensed root of which a bulb of flesh would swell, squeezing out one tawny globe, then another, a third, after which the folds of black skin would close again and the tail droop.

In the victoria sat, with her legs crossed, Peter's sister, a dark-complexioned young lady (although only nineteen, she had already divorced one husband), in a bright frock, high-laced white boots with glistening black caps, and a wide-brimmed hat that cast a lacy shadow upon her face. Ever since morning she had been in a vile temper, and now, when Peter turned to her for the third time, she directed at him the point of her iridescent parasol and said: "Stop fidgeting, please."

The first part of the way went through the woods. Splendid clouds gliding across the blue only increased the glitter and vivacity of the summer day. If one looked from below at the tops of the birches, their verdure reminded one of sun-soaked translucent grapes. On both sides of the road bushes exposed the pale underside of their leaves to the hot wind. Shine and shade speckled the depths of the forest: one could not separate the pattern of tree trunks from that of their interspaces. Here and there a patch of moss flashed its heavenly emerald. Floppy ferns ran past, almost brushing against the wheels.

There appeared in front a great wagon of hay, a greenish mountain flecked with tremulous light. Stepan reined in his steeds; the mountain inclined over to one side, the carriage to the other—there was barely room enough to pass on the narrow forest road—and one caught a tangy whiff of new-mown fields, and the ponderous creak of cartwheels, and a glimpse of wilted scabiouses and daisies amidst the hay, and then Stepan clicked his tongue, gave a shake to his reins, and the wagon was left behind. Presently the woods parted, the victoria turned onto the highway, and farther came harvested fields, the stridulation of grasshoppers in the ditches and the humming of telegraph poles. In a moment the village of Voskresensk would show up, and a few minutes later it would be the end.

"Plead sickness? Topple down from the box?" glumly wondered Peter as the first izbas appeared.

His tightish white shorts hurt in the crotch, his brown shoes pinched dreadfully, he felt nasty qualms in his stomach. The afternoon awaiting him was oppressive, repulsive—and inevitable.

They were now driving through the village, and somewhere from behind the fences and log cabins a wooden echo responded to the harmonious plashing of hooves. On the clayey, grass-patched side of the road peasant boys were playing *gorodki*—pitching stout sticks at wooden pins which resoundingly flew up in the air. Peter recognized the stuffed hawk and silvered spheres that ornamented the garden of the local grocer. A dog dashed out of a gateway, in perfect silence—storing up voice, as it were—and only after flying across the ditch, and finally overtaking the carriage, did it peal forth its bark. Shakily straddling a shaggy nag a peasant rode by, his elbows widely parted, his shirt, with a tear on the shoulder, ballooning in the wind.

At the end of the village, on a hillock thickly crested with limes, stood a red church and, next to it, a smaller mausoleum of white stone and pyramidal shape, thus resembling a cream paskha. The river came into view; with the green brocade of aquatic flora coating it at the bend. Close to the sloping highway stood a squat smithy, on the wall of which someone had chalked: Long Live Serbia! The sound of the hooves suddenly acquired a ringing, resilient tone—because of the boards of the bridge over which the carriage passed. A barefoot old angler stood leaning against the railing; a tin receptacle gleamed at his ankle. Presently the sound of the hooves turned to a soft thudding: the bridge, the fisherman, and the riverbend dropped back irremediably.

The victoria was now rolling along a dusty, fluffy road between two rows of stout-trunked birches. In an instant, yes, in an instant, from behind its park the green roof of the Kozlovs' manorhouse would loom. Peter knew by experience how awkward and revolting it would be. He was ready to give away his new "Swift" bicycle—and what else in the bargain?—well, the steel bow, say, and the "Pugach" pistol and all its supply of powder-stuffed corks, in order to be back again in the ancestral domain ten versts from here, and to spend the summer day as always, in solitary, marvelous games.

From the park came a dark, damp reek of mushrooms and firs. Then appeared a corner of the house and the brick-red sand in front of the stone porch.

"The children are in the garden," said Mrs. Kozlov, when Peter and his sister, having traversed several cool rooms redolent of carnations, reached the main veranda where a number of grown-ups were assembled. Peter said how-do-you-do to each, scraping, and making sure not to kiss a man's hand by mistake as had once happened. His sister kept her palm on the top of his head—something she never did at home. Then she settled in a wicker armchair and became unusually animated. Everybody started talking at once. Mrs. Kozlov took Peter by the wrist, led him down a short flight of steps between tubbed laurels and oleanders, and with an air of mystery pointed gardenward: "You will find them there," she said; "go and join them"; whereupon she returned to her guests. Peter remained standing on the lower step.

A rotten beginning. He now had to walk across the garden terrace and penetrate into an avenue where, in spotted sunshine, voices throbbed and colors flickered. One had to accomplish that journey all alone, coming ever nearer, endlessly nearer, while entering gradually the visual field of many eyes.

It was the name-day of Mrs. Kozlov's eldest son, Vladimir, a lively and teasy lad of Peter's age. There was also Vladimir's brother Constantine, and their two sisters, Baby and Lola. From the adjacent estate a pony-drawn *sharabanchik* brought the two young Barons Korff and their sister Tanya, a pretty girl of eleven or twelve with an ivory pale skin, bluish shadows under the eyes, and a black braid caught by a white bow above her delicate neck. In addition there were three schoolboys in their summer uniforms and Vasiliy Tuchkov, a robust, well-built, suntanned thirteen-year-old cousin of Peter's. The games were directed by Elenski, a university student, the tutor of the Kozlov boys. He was a fleshy, plump-chested young man with a shaven head. He wore a *kosovorotka*, a shirtlike affair with side buttons on the collar bone. A rimless pince-nez surmounted his nose, whose chiseled sharpness did not suit at all the soft ovality of his face. When finally Peter approached, he found Elenski and the children in the act of throwing javelins at a large target of painted straw nailed to a fir trunk.

Peter's last visit to the Kozlovs had been in St. Petersburg at Easter and on that occasion magic-lantern slides had been shown. Elenski read aloud Lermontov's poem about Mtsyri, a young monk who left his Caucasian retreat to roam among the mountains, and a fellow student handled the lantern. In the middle of a luminous circle on the damp sheet there would appear (stopping there after a spasmodic incursion) a colored picture: Mtsyri and the snow leopard attacking him. Elenski, interrupting the reading for a minute, would point out with a short stick first the young monk and then the leaping leopard, and as he did so, the stick borrowed the picture's colors which would then slip off his wand when Elenski removed it. Each illustration tarried for quite a time on the sheet as only some ten slides were assigned to the long-winded epic. Vasiliy Tuchkov now and then raised his hand in the dark, reached up to the ray, and five black fingers spread out on the sheet. Once or twice the assistant inserted a slide the wrong way, topsyturvying the picture. Tuchkov roared with laughter, but Peter was embarrassed for the assistant, and, in general, did his best to feign enormous interest. That time, too, he first met Tanya Korff and since then often thought about her, imagining himself saving her from highwaymen, with Vasiliy Tuchkov helping him and devotedly admiring his courage (it was rumored that Vasiliy had a real revolver at home, with a mother-of-pearl grip).

At present, his brown legs set wide, his left hand loosely placed on the chainlet of his cloth belt which had a small canvas purse on one side, Vasiliy was aiming the javelin at the target. He swung back his throwing arm, he hit the bull's-eye, and Elenski uttered a loud "bravo." Peter carefully pulled out the spear, quietly walked back to Vasiliy's former position, quietly took aim and also hit the white, red-ringed center; no one, however, witnessed this as the competition was over by now and busy preparations for another game had begun. A kind of low cabinet or whatnot had been dragged into the avenue and set up there on the sand. Its top had several round holes and a fat frog of metal with a wide-open mouth. A large leaden counter had to be cast in such a way as to pop into one of the holes or enter the gaping green mouth. The counter fell through the holes or the mouth into numbered compartments on the shelves below; the frog's mouth gave one five hundred points, each of the other holes one hundred or less depending on its distance from *la grenouille* (a Swiss governess had imported the game). The players took turns in throwing one by one several counters, and marks were laboriously written down on the sand. The whole affair was rather tedious, and between turns some of the players sought the bilberry jungle under the trees of the park. The berries were big, with a bloom dimming their blue, which revealed a bright violet luster if touched by beslavered fingers. Peter, squatting on his haunches and gently grunting, would accumulate the berries in his cupped hand and then transfer the entire handful to his mouth. That way it tasted particularly good. Sometimes a serrate little leaf got mixed up in one's mouth with the fruit. Vasiliy Tuchkov found a small caterpillar, with varicolored tufts of hair along its back in toothbrush arrangement, and calmly swallowed it to the general admiration. A woodpecker was tapping nearby; heavy bumblebees droned above the undergrowth and crawled into the pale bending corollas of boyar bellflowers. From the avenue came the clatter of cast counters and the stentorian, r-trilling voice of Elenski advising somebody to "keep trying." Tanya crouched next to Peter, and with her pale face expressing the greatest attention, her glistening purple lips parted, groped for the berries. Peter silently offered her his hand-cupped collection, she graciously accepted it, and he started to gather a new helping for her. Presently however, came her turn to play, and she ran back to the avenue, lifting high her slim legs in white stockings.

The *grenouille* game was becoming a universal bore. Some dropped out, others played haphazardly; as to Vasiliy

Tuchkov, he went and hurled a stone at the gaping frog, and everybody laughed, except Elenski and Peter. The *imeninnik* ("name-dayer"), handsome, charming, merry Vladimir, now demanded that they play at *palochka-stuka-lochka* ("knock-knock stick"). The Korff boys joined in his request. Tanya skipped on one foot, applauding.

"No, no children, impossible," said Elenski. "In half an hour or so we shall go to a picnic; it is a long drive, and colds are caught quickly if one is all hot from running."

"Oh, please, please," cried the children.

"Please," softly repeated Peter after the others, deciding he would manage to share a hiding place either with Vasiliy or Tanya.

"I am forced to grant the general request," said Elenski, who was prone to round out his utterings; "I do not see, however, the necessary implement." Vladimir sped off to borrow it from a flowerbed.

Peter went up to a seesaw on which stood Tanya, Lola, and Vasiliy; the latter kept jumping and stamping, making the plank creak and jerk while the girls squealed, trying to keep their balance.

"I'm falling, I'm falling!" exclaimed Tanya, and both she and Lola jumped down on the grass.

"Would you like some more bilberries?" asked Peter.

She shook her head, then looked askance at Lola, and, turning to Peter again, added: "She and I have decided to stop speaking to you."

"But why?" mumbled Peter, flushing painfully.

"Because you are a poseur," replied Tanya, and jumped back onto the seesaw. Peter pretended to be deeply engrossed in the examination of a frizzly-black molehill on the edge of the avenue.

In the meantime a panting Vladimir had brought the

"necessary implement"—a green sharp little stick, of the sort used by gardeners to prop up peonies and dahlias but also very much like Elenski's wand at the magic-lantern show. It remained to be settled who would be the "knocker."

"One. Two. Three. Four," began Elenski in a comic narrative tone, while pointing the stick at every player in turn. "The rabbit. Peeped out. Of his door. A hunter. Alas" (Elenski paused and sneezed powerfully). "Happened to pass" (the narrator replaced his pince-nez). "And his gun. Went bang. Bang. And. The. Poor" (the syllables grew more and more stressed and spaced). "Hare. Died. There."

The "there" fell on Peter. But all the other children crowded around Elenski, clamoring for him to be the seeker. One could hear them exclaiming: "Please, please, it will be much more fun!"

"All right, I consent," replied Elenski, without even glancing at Peter.

At the point where the avenue joined the garden terrace, there stood a whitewashed, partly peeled bench with a barred back, also white and also peeling. It was on this bench that Elenski sat down with the green stick in his hands. He humped his fat shoulders, closed his eyes tight and started to count aloud to one hundred, giving time to the players to hide. Vasiliy and Tanya, as if acting in collusion, disappeared in the depths of the park. One of the uniformed schoolboys cannily placed himself behind a linden trunk, only three yards away from the bench. Peter, after a wistful glance at the speckled shade of the shrubbery, turned away and went in the opposite direction, toward the house: he planned to ambuscade on the veranda —not on the main one, of course, where the grown-ups were having tea to the sound of a brass-horned gramophone

singing in Italian, but on a lateral porch giving on Elenski's bench. Luckily, it turned out to be empty. The various colors of the panes inset in its latticed casements were
reflected beneath on the long narrow divans, upholstered in
dove-gray with exaggerated roses, that lined the walls.
There were also a bentwood rocking chair, a dog's bowl,
licked clean, on the floor, and an oilcloth-covered table
with nothing upon it save a lone-looking pair of old-person
spectacles.

Peter crept up to the many-colored window and kneeled
on a cushion under the white ledge. At some distance one
saw a coral-pink Elenski sitting on a coral-pink bench
under the ruby-black leaves of a linden. The rule was that
the "seeker," when leaving his post to spy out the concealed
players, should also leave his stick behind. Wariness and a
nice judgment of pace and place, advised him not to stray
too far, lest a player make a sudden dash from an unsighted
point and reach the bench before the "seeker" could get
back to it and give a rap of victory with the regained wand.
Peter's plan was simple: as soon as Elenski, having finished
counting, put the stick down on the bench, and set off
toward the shrubbery with its most likely lurking spots,
Peter would sprint from his veranda to the bench and give
it the sacramental "knock-knock" with the unguarded stick.
About half a minute had already elapsed. A light-blue Elenski sat hunched up under indigo-black foliage and tapped
his toe on the silver-blue sand in rhythm with the count.
How delightful it would have been to wait thus, and peer
through this or that lozenge of stained glass, if only Tanya
... Oh, why? What did I do to her?

The number of plain-glass panes was much inferior to
that of the rest. A gray and white wagtail walked past
across the sand-colored sand. There were bits of cobweb

in the corners of the latticework. On the ledge a dead fly lay on its back. A bright-yellow Elenski rose from his golden bench and gave a warning knock. At the same instant, the door leading on to the veranda from the inside of the house opened, and out of the dusk of a room there came first a corpulent brown dachshund and then a gray bobhaired little old woman in a tight-belted black dress with a trefoil-shaped brooch on her chest and a chainlet around her neck connecting with the watch stuck into her belt. Very indolently, sideways, the dog descended the steps into the garden. As to the old lady she angrily snatched up the spectacles—for which she had come. All of a sudden she noticed the boy crawling off his seat.

"*Priate-qui? Priate-qui?* (*pryatki*, hide-and-seek)," she uttered with the farcical accent inflicted on Russian by old Frenchwomen after half a century of life in our country. "*Toute n'est caroche* (*tut ne khorosho*, here not good)," she continued, considering with kindly eyes Peter's face that expressed both embarrassment with his situation and entreaty not to speak too loud. "*Sichasse pocajou caroche messt*" (*seychas pokazhu khoroshee mesto*, right away I'll show a good place).

An emerald Elenski stood with arms akimbo on the pale green sand and kept glancing in all directions at once. Peter, fearing the creaky and fussy voice of the old governess might be heard outside, and fearing even more to offend her by a refusal, hastened to follow her, though quite conscious of the ludicrous turn things were taking. Holding him firmly by the hand she led him through one room after another, past a white piano, past a card table, past a little tricycle, and as the variety of sudden objects increased— elk antlers, bookcases, a decoy duck on a shelf—he felt she was taking him to the opposite side of the house and making it more and more difficult to explain, without hurting her, that the game she had interrupted was not so much a matter of hiding as of awaiting the moment when Elenski would retreat sufficiently far from the bench to allow one to run to it and knock upon it with the all-important stick!

After passing through a succession of rooms, they turned into a corridor, then went up a flight of stairs, then traversed a sunlit mangleroom where a rosy-cheeked woman sat knitting on a trunk near the window: she looked up, smiled and lowered her lashes again, her knitting needles never stopping. The old governess led Peter into the next room where stood a leathern couch and an empty bird's cage and where there was a dark niche between a huge mahogany wardrobe and a Dutch stove.

"*Votte* (here you are)," said the old lady, and having pressed him with a light push into that hiding place, went back to the mangleroom, where in her garbled Russian she continued a gossipy conversation with the comely knitter who kept inserting every now and then an automatic "*Skazhite pozhaluysta!* (Well, I never)."

For a while Peter remained kneeling politely in his absurd nook; presently he straightened up, but continued standing there and peering at the wallpaper with its blandly indifferent azure scroll, at the window, at the top of a poplar rippling in the sun. One could hear a clock hoarsely ticktocking and that sound reminded one of various dull and sad things.

A lot of time passed. The conversation in the next room began to move away and to lose itself in the distance. Now all was silent, except the clock. Peter emerged from his niche.

He ran down the stairs, tiptoed rapidly through the rooms (bookcases, elkhorns, tricycle, blue card table, piano) and was met at the open door leading to the veranda by a pattern of colored sun and by the old dog returning from the garden. Peter stole up to the windowpanes and chose an unstained one. On the white bench lay the green wand. Elenski was invisible—he had walked off, no doubt, in his unwary search, far beyond the lindens that lined the avenue.

Grinning from sheer excitement, Peter skipped down the steps and rushed toward the bench. He was still running, when he noted an odd irresponsiveness around him. However, at the same swift pace he reached the bench and knocked its seat thrice with the stick. A vain gesture. Nobody appeared. Flecks of sunlight pulsated on the sand. A ladybird was walking up a bench arm, the transparent tips of her carelessly folded wings showing untidily from under her small spotted cupola.

Peter waited for a minute or two, stealing glances around, and finally realized that he had been forgotten, that the existence of a last, unfound, unflushed lurker had been overlooked, and that everybody had gone to the picnic without him. That picnic, incidentally, had been for him the only acceptable promise of the day: he had been looking forward after a fashion to it, to the absence of grownups there, to the fire built in a forest clearing, to the baked potatoes, to the bilberry tarts, to the iced tea in thermos bottles. The picnic was now snatched away, but one could reconcile oneself to that privation. What rankled was something else.

Peter swallowed hard and still holding the green stick wandered back to the house. Uncles, aunts, and their friends were playing cards on the main veranda; he distinguished the sound of his sister's laughter—a nasty sound. He walked around the mansion, with the vague thought that somewhere near it there must be a lily pond and that he might leave on its brink his monogrammed handkerchief and his silver whistle on its white cord, while he himself would go, unnoticed, all the way home. Suddenly, near the pump behind a corner of the house he heard a familiar burst of voices. All were there—Elenski, Vasiliy, Tanya, her brothers and cousins; they clustered around a peasant who was showing a baby owl he had just found. The owlet, a fat little thing, brown, white-speckled, kept shifting this way and that its head or rather its facial disc, for one could not make out exactly where the head started and the body stopped.

Peter approached. Vasiliy Tuchkov glanced at him and said to Tanya with a chuckle:

"And here comes the poseur."

ORACHE

Lebeda *was first published in* Poslednie Novosti, Paris, January *31, 1932; collected in* Soglyadatay, Russkiya Zapiski, Paris, *1938.* "Lebeda" *is the plant* Atriplex. *Its English name, orache, by a miraculous coincidence, renders in its written form the* "ili beda," "or ache," *suggested by the Russian title. Through the rearranged patterns of the story, readers of my* Speak, Memory *will recognize many details of the final section of Chapter Nine,* Speak, Memory, *1966, Putnam's, New York. Amidst the mosaic of fiction there are some real memories not represented in* Speak, Memory, *such as the passages about the teacher* "Berezovski" (Berezin, *a popular geographer of the day), including the fight with the school bully. The place is St. Petersburg, the time around 1910.*

The vastest room in their St. Petersburg mansion was the library. There, before the drive to school, Peter would look in to say good morning to his father. Crepitations of steel and the scraping of soles: every morning his father fenced with Monsieur Mascara, a diminutive elderly Frenchman made of gutta-percha and black bristle. On Sundays Mascara came to teach Peter gymnastics and pugilism—and usually interrupted the lesson because of dyspepsia: through secret passages, through canyons of bookcases, through deep dim corridors, he retreated for half an hour to one of the water closets on the first floor. Peter, his thin hot wrists thrust into huge boxing gloves, waited, sprawling in a leather armchair, listening to the light buzz of silence, and blinking to ward off somnolence. The lamplight, which on winter mornings seemed always of a dull tawny tint, shone on the rosined linoleum, on the shelves lining the walls, on the defenseless spines of books huddling there in tight ranks, and on the black gallows of a pear-shaped punching ball. Beyond the plate-glass windows, soft slow snow kept densely falling with a kind of monotonous and sterile grace.

At school, recently, the geography teacher, Berezovski (author of a booklet "*Chao-San, the Land of the Morning*: Korea and Koreans, with thirteen illustrations and a map in the text"), fingering his dark little beard, informed the entire class, unexpectedly and malapropos, that Mascara was giving Peter and him private lessons in boxing. Everybody stared at Peter. Embarrassment caused Peter's face to glow brightly and even to become somewhat puffy. At the next recess, Shchukin, his strongest, roughest, and most backward classmate came up to him and said with a grin: "Come on, show how you box." "Leave me alone," replied Peter gently. Shchukin emitted a nasal grunt and hit Peter in the underbelly. Peter resented this. With a straight left, as taught by Monsieur Mascara, he bloodied Shchukin's nose. A stunned pause, red spots on a handkerchief. Having recovered from his astonishment, Shchukin fell upon Peter and started to maul him. Though his whole body hurt, Peter felt satisfied. Blood from Shchukin's nose continued to flow throughout the lesson of Natural History, stopped during Sums, and retrickled at Sacred Studies. Peter watched with quiet interest.

That winter Peter's mother took Mara to Mentone. Mara was sure she was dying of consumption. The absence of his sister, a rather badgering young lady with a caustic tongue, did not displease Peter, but he could not get over his mother's departure; he missed her terribly, especially in the evenings. He never saw much of his father. His father was busy in a place known as the Parliament (where a couple of years earlier the ceiling had collapsed). There was also something called the Kadet Party, which had nothing to do with parties or cadets. Very often Peter would have to dine separately upstairs, with Miss Sheldon—who had black hair and blue eyes and wore a knit tie with transverse stripes over her voluminous blouse—while downstairs near the monstrously swollen hall stands fully fifty pairs of rubbers would accumulate; and if he passed from the vestibule to the side room with its silk-covered Turkish divan he could suddenly hear—when somewhere in the distance a footman opened a door—a cacophonic din, a zoolike hubbub, and the remote but clear voice of his father.

One gloomy November morning Dmitri Korff, who shared a school desk with Peter, took out of his piebald satchel and handed to him a cheap satirical magazine. On one of the first pages there was a cartoon—with green color predominating—depicting Peter's father and accompanied by a jingle. Glancing at the lines, Peter caught a fragment from the middle:

> *V syom stolknovenii neschastnom*
> *Kak dzentelmen on predlagal*
> *Revolver, sablyu il' kinzhal.*

> (In this unfortunate affray
> He offered like a gentleman
> Revolver, dagger, or épée.)

"Is it true?" asked Dmitri in a whisper (the lesson had just begun). "What do you mean—true?" whispered Peter back. "Pipe down, you two," broke in Aleksey Matveich, the teacher of Russian, a muzhik-looking man, with an impediment in his speech, a nondescript and untidy growth above a crooked lip and celebrated legs in screwy trousers: when he walked his feet tangled—he set the right one where the left should have landed and vice-versa—but nevertheless his progress was extremely rapid. He now sat at his table and leafed through his little notebook; presently his eyes focused on a distant desk, from behind which, like a tree grown by the glance of a fakir, Shchukin was rising.

"What do you mean—true?" softly repeated Peter, holding the magazine in his lap and looking askance at Dmitri. Dmitri moved a little closer to him. Meanwhile, Shchukin, crop-headed, wearing a Russian blouse of black serge, was beginning for the third time, with a sort of hopeless zest: "*Mumu*... Turgenev's story *Mumu*..." "That bit about your father," answered Dmitri in a low voice. Aleksey Matveich banged the *Zhivoe Slovo* (a school anthology) against the table with such violence that a pen jumped and stuck its nib in the floor. "What's going on there? ... What's this ... you whisperers?" spoke the teacher, spitting out sibilant words incoherently: "Stand up, stand up.... Korff, Shishkov.... What is it you're doing there?" He advanced and nimbly snatched away the magazine. "So you're reading smut ... sit down, sit down ... smut." His booty he put into his briefcase.

Next, Peter was called to the blackboard. He was told to write out the first line of a poem which he was supposed to have learned by heart. He wrote:

> ... *uzkoyu mezhoy*
> *Porosshey kashkoyu ... ili bedoy ...*
>
> (... along a narrow margin overgrown
> with clover ... or ache ...)

Here came a shout so jarring that Peter dropped his bit of chalk:

"What are you scrawling? Why *bedoy*, when it's *lebedoy*, orache—a clingy weed? Where are your thoughts roaming? Go back to your seat!"

"Well, is it true?" asked Dmitri in a well-timed whisper. Peter pretended he did not hear. He could not stop the shiver running through him; in his ears there kept echoing the verse about the "revolver, dagger, or épée"; he kept seeing before him the sharp-angled pale-green caricature of his father, with the green crossing the outline in one place and not reaching it in another—a negligence of the color print. Quite recently, before his ride to school, that crepitation of steel, that scrape of soles ... his father and the fencing master, both wearing padded chest protectors and wire-mesh masks.... It had all been so habitual—the Frenchman's uvular cries, *rompez, battez!*, the robust movements of his father, the flicker and clink of the foils.... A pause: panting and smiling, he removed the convex mask from his damp pink face.

The lesson ended. Aleksey Matveich carried away the magazine. Chalk-pale, Peter kept sitting where he was, lifting and lowering the lid of his desk. His classmates, with deferential curiosity, clustered around him, pressing him for details. He knew nothing and tried himself to discover something from the shower of questions. What he could make out was that Tumanski, a fellow member of the Parliament, had aspersed his father's honor and his father had challenged him to a duel.

Two more lessons dragged by, then came the main recess, with snowball fights in the yard. For no reason at all Peter began stuffing his snowballs with frozen earth, something he had never done before. In the course of the next lesson Nussbaum, the German teacher, lost his temper and roared at Shchukin (who was having bad luck that day), and Peter felt a spasm in his throat and asked leave to go to the toilet—so as not to burst into tears in public. There, in solitary suspension near the washbowl, was the unbelievably soiled, unbelievably slimy towel—more exactly the corpse of a towel that had passed through many wet, hastily kneading hands. For a minute or so Peter looked at himself in the glass—the best method of keeping the face from dissolving in a grimace of crying.

He wondered if he should not leave for home before three o'clock, the regular time, but chased that thought away. Self-control, the motto is self-control! The storm in class had subsided. Shchukin, scarlet-eared but absolutely calm, was back in his place, sitting there with his arms folded crosswise.

One more lesson—and then the final bell, which differed in sustained hoarse emphasis from those that marked the earlier periods. Arctics, short fur coat, *shapska* with earflaps, were quickly slipped on, and Peter ran across the yard, penetrated into its tunnellike exit, and jumped over the dogboard of the gate. No automobile had been sent to fetch him, so he had to take a hackney sleigh. The driver, lean-bottomed, flat-backed, perching slightly askew on his low seat, had an eccentric way of urging his horse on: he would pretend to draw the knout out of the leg of his long boot, or else his hand adumbrated a kind of beckoning gesture directed to no one in particular, and then the sleigh jerked, causing the pencil case to rattle in Peter's satchel, and it was all dully oppressive and increased his anxiety, and oversize, irregularly shaped, hastily modeled snowflakes fell upon the sleazy sleighrobe.

At home, since the departure of his mother and sister, afternoons were quiet. Peter went up the wide, gentle-graded staircase where on the second landing stood a table of green malachite with a vase for visiting cards, presided over by a replica of the Venus of Milo that his cousins had once rigged up in a plush-velveteen coat and a hat with sham cherries, whereupon she began to resemble Praskovia Stepanovna, an impoverished widow who would call every first of the month. Peter reached the upper floor and hallooed his governess's name. But Miss Sheldon had a guest for tea, the English governess of the Veretennikovs. Miss Sheldon sent Peter to prepare his school tasks for the next morning. Not forgetting first to wash his hands and drink his glass of milk. Her door closed. Peter, feeling smothered in cotton-woollish, ghastly anguish, dawdled in the nursery, then descended to the second floor and peeped into his father's study. The silence there was unendurable. Then a crisp sound broke it—the fall of an incurved chrysanthemum petal. On the monumental writing desk the familiar, discreetly gleaming objects were fixed in an orderly cosmic array, like planets: cabinet photographs, a marble egg, a majestic inkstand.

Peter passed into his mother's boudoir, and thence into its oriel and stood there for quite a while looking through an elongated casement. It was almost night by that time, at that latitude. Around the globes of lilac-tinted lights the snowflakes fluttered. Below, the black outlines of sleighs with the silhouettes of hunched-up passengers flowed hazily. Maybe next morning? It always takes place in the morning, very early.

He walked down to the first floor. A silent wilderness. In the library, with nervous haste, he switched on the light and the black shadows swept away. Having settled down in a nook near one of the bookcases, he tried to occupy his mind with the examination of the huge bound volumes of the *Zhivopisnoe obozrenie* (a Russian counterpart of *The Graphic*). Masculine beauty depends on a splendid beard and a sumptuous mustache. Since girlhood I suffered from blackheads. Concert accordion "Pleasure," with 20 voices and 10 valves. A group of priests and a wooden church. A painting with the legend "Strangers": gentleman moping at his writing desk, lady with curly boa standing some distance away in the act of gloving her wide-fingered hand. I've already looked at this volume. He pulled out another and instantly was confronted by the picture of a duel between two Italian swordsmen: one lunges madly, the other sidesteps the thrust and pierces his opponent's throat. Peter slammed the heavy tome shut, and froze, holding his temples like a grown-up. Everything was frightening—the stillness, the motionless bookcases, the glossy dumbbells on an oaken table, the black boxes of the card index. With bent head he sped like the wind through murky rooms. Back again in the nursery, he lay down on a couch and remained lying there until Miss Sheldon remembered his existence. From the stairs came the sound of the dinner gong.

As Peter was on his way down, his father came out of his study, accompanied by Colonel Rozen, who had once been engaged to the long-dead young sister of Peter's father. Peter dared not glance at his father and when the latter's large palm, emitting familiar warmth, touched the side of his son's head, Peter blushed to the point of tears. It was impossible, unbearable, to think that this man, the best person on earth, was going to duel with some dim *Enigmanski*. Using what weapons? Pistols? Swords? Why does nobody talk about it? Do the servants know? The governess? Mother in Mentone? At table the colonel joked as he always did, abruptly, briefly, as if cracking nuts, but tonight Peter instead of laughing was suffused with blushes, which he tried to conceal by deliberately dropping his napkin so as to rally quietly under the table and regain there his normal complexion, but he would crawl out even redder than before and his father would raise his eyebrows —and merrily, unhurriedly, with characteristic evenness perfom the rites of eating dinner, of carefully quaffing wine from a low golden cup with a handle. Colonel Rozen went on cracking jokes. Miss Sheldon, who had no Russian, kept silent, sternly protruding her chest; and whenever

Peter hunched his back she would give him a nasty poke under the shoulder blades. For dessert there was pistachio parfait, which he loathed.

After dinner, his father and the colonel went up to the study. Peter looked so queer that his father asked: "What's the matter? Why are you sulking?" And miraculously Peter managed to answer distinctly: "No, I'm not sulking." Miss Sheldon led him bedward. As soon as the light was extinguished, he buried his face in the pillow. Onegin shed his cloak, Lenski plopped down on the boards like a black sack. One could see the point of the épée coming out at the back of the Italian's neck. Mascara liked to tell about the *rencontre* which he had had in his youth: half a centimeter lower—and the liver would have been pierced. And the homework for tomorrow has not been done, and the darkness in the bedroom is total, and he must get up early, very early, better not shut my eyes or I'll oversleep—the thing is sure to be scheduled for tomorrow. Oh, I'll skip school, I'll skip it, I'll say—sore throat. Mother will be back only at Christmas. Mentone, blue picture postcards. Must insert the latest one in my album. One corner has now gone in, the next——

Peter woke up as usual, around eight, as usual he heard a ringing sound: that was the servant responsible for the stoves—he had opened a damper. With his hair still wet after a hasty bath, Peter went downstairs and found his father boxing with Mascara as if it were an ordinary day. "Sore throat?" he said, repeating it after Peter. "Yes, a scrapy feeling," said Peter speaking low. "Look here, are you telling the truth?" Peter felt that all further explanations were perilous: the floodgate was about to burst, liberating a disgraceful torrent. He silently turned away and presently was seated in the limousine with his satchel in his lap. He felt queasy. Everything was horrible and irremediable.

Somehow or other he managed to be late for the first lesson, and stood for a long time with his hand raised behind the glazed door of his class but was not permitted to enter and went roaming about in the hall, and then hoisted himself onto a window ledge with the vague idea of doing his tasks but did not get farther than:

... with clover and with clinging orache

and for the thousandth time began imagining the way it would all happen—in the mist of a frosty dawn. How should he go about discovering the date agreed upon? How could he find out the details? Had he been in the last form —no, even in the last but one—he might have suggested: Let me take your place.

Finally the bell rang. A noisy crowd filled the recreation hall. He heard Dmitri Korff's voice in sudden proximity: "Well, are you glad? Are you glad?" Peter looked at him with dull perplexity. "Andrey downstairs has a newspaper," said Dmitri excitedly. "Come, we have just got time, you'll see—But what's the matter? If I were you——"

In the vestibule, on his stool, sat Andrey the old porter, reading. He raised his eyes and smiled. "It is all here, all written down here," said Dmitri. Peter took the paper and made out through a trembling blur: "Yesterday in the early afternoon, on Krestovski Island, G. D. Shishkov and Count A. S. Tumanski fought a duel, the outcome of which was fortunately bloodless. Count Tumanski, who fired first, missed, whereupon his opponent discharged his pistol into the air. The seconds were——"

And then the floodgate broke. The porter and Dmitri Korff attempted to calm him, but he kept pushing them away, shaken by spasms, his face concealed, he could not breathe, never before had he known such tears, do not tell anyone, please, I am simply not very well, I have this pain —and again a tumult of sobs.

THE RETURN OF CHORB

First published in two issues of the Russian émigré Rul' (*Berlin*), *November 12 and 13, 1925. Reprinted in the collection* Vozvrash-chenie Chorba, Slovo, Berlin, *1930.*

An English version by Gleb Struve (The Return of Tchorb *by Vladimir Sirin*) *appeared in the anthology* This Quarter (*Vol. IV, No. 4, June, 1932*) *published in Paris by Edw. W. Titus. After rereading that version forty years later I was sorry to find it too tame in style and too inaccurate in sense for my present purpose. I have retranslated the story completely in collaboration with my son.*

It was written not long after my novel Mashenka (*Mary*) *was finished and is a good example of my early constructions. The place is a small town in Germany half a century ago. I notice that the road from Nice to Grasse where I imagined poor Mrs. Chorb walking was still unpaved and chalky with dust around 1920. I have skipped her mother's ponderous name and patronymic "Varvara Klimovna," which would have meant nothing to my Anglo-American readers.*

The Kellers left the opera house at a late hour. In that pacific German city, where the very air seemed a little lusterless and where a transverse row of ripples had kept shading gently the reflected cathedral for well over seven centuries, Wagner was a leisurely affair presented with relish so as to overgorge one with music. After the opera Keller took his wife to a smart nightclub renowned for its white wine. It was past one in the morning when their car, flippantly lit on the inside, sped through lifeless streets to deposit them at the iron wicket of their small but dignified private house. Keller, a thickset old German, closely resembling Oom Paul Kruger, was the first to step down on the sidewalk, across which the loopy shadows of leaves stirred in the streetlamp's gray glimmer. For an instant his starched shirt front and the droplets of bugles trimming his wife's dress caught the light as she disengaged a stout leg and climbed out of the car in her turn. The maid met them in the vestibule and, still carried by the momentum of the news, told them in a frightened whisper about Chorb's having called. Frau Keller's chubby face, whose everlasting freshness somehow agreed with her Russian merchant-class parentage, quivered and reddened with agitation.

"He said she was ill?"

The maid whispered still faster. Keller stroked his gray

brush of hair with his fat palm, and an old man's frown overcast his large, somewhat simian face, with its long upper lip and deep furrows.

"I simply refuse to wait till tomorrow," muttered Frau Keller shaking her head as she gyrated heavily on one spot, trying to catch the end of the veil that covered her auburn wig. "We'll go there at once. Oh dear, or dear! No wonder there's been no letters for quite a month."

Keller punched his gibus open and said in his precise, slightly guttural Russian:

"The man is insane. How dare he, if she's ill, take her a second time to that vile hotel?"

But they were wrong, of course, in thinking that their daughter was ill. Chorb said so to the maid only because it was easier to utter. In point of fact he had returned alone from abroad and only now realized that, like it or not, he would have to explain how his wife had perished, and why he had written nothing about it to his in-laws. It was all very difficult. How was he to explain that he wished to possess his grief all by himself, without tainting it by any foreign substance and without sharing it with any other soul? Her death appeared to him as a most rare, almost unheard-of occurrence; nothing, it seemed to him, could be purer than such a death, caused by the impact of an electric stream, the same stream which, when poured into glass receptacles, yields the purest and brightest light.

Ever since that spring day when, on the white highway a dozen kilometers from Nice, she had touched, laughing, the live wire of a storm-felled pole, Chorb's entire world ceased to sound like a world: it retreated at once, and even the dead body that he carried in his arms to the nearest village struck him as something alien and needless.

In Nice, where she had to be buried, the disagreeable

consumptive clergyman kept in vain pressing him for details: Chorb responded only with a languid smile. He sat daylong on the shingly beach, cupping colored pebbles and letting them flow from hand to hand; and then, suddenly, without waiting for the funeral, he traveled back to Germany.

He passed in reverse through all the spots they had visited together during their honeymoon journey. In Switzerland where they had wintered and where the apple trees were now in their last bloom, he recognized nothing except the hotels. As to the Black Forest, through which they had hiked in the preceding autumn, the chill of the spring did not impede memory. And just as he had tried, on the southern beach, to find again that unique rounded black pebble with the regular little white belt, which she had happened to show him on the eve of their last ramble, so now he did his best to look up all the roadside items that retained her exclamation mark: the special profile of a cliff, a hut roofed with a layer of silvery-gray scales, a black fir tree and a footbridge over a white torrent, and something which one might be inclined to regard as a kind of fatidic prefiguration: the radial span of a spider's web between two telegraph wires that were beaded with droplets of mist. She accompanied him: her little boots stepped rapidly, and her hands never stopped moving, moving—to pluck a leaf from a bush or stroke a rock wall in passing—light, laughing hands that knew no repose. He saw her small face with its dense dark freckles, and her wide eyes, whose pale greenish hue was that of the shards of glass licked smooth by the sea waves. He thought that if he managed to gather all the little things they had noticed together—if he re-created thus the near past—her image would grow immortal and replace her for ever. Nighttime, though, was unendurable. Night imbued with sudden terror her irrational presence. He hardly slept at all during the three weeks of his trek—and now he got off, quite drugged with fatigue, at the railway station, which had been last autumn their point of departure from the quiet town where he had met and married her.

It was around eight o'clock of the evening. Beyond the houses the cathedral tower was sharply set off in black against a golden-red stripe of sunset. In the station square stood in file the selfsame decrepit fiacres. The identical newspaper seller uttered his hollow crepuscular cry. The same black poodle with apathetic eyes was in the act of raising a thin hindleg near a Morris pillar, straight at the scarlet lettering of a playbill announcing *Parsifal*.

Chorb's luggage consisted of a suitcase and a big tawny trunk. A fiacre took him through the town. The cabby kept indolently flapping his reins, while steadying the trunk with one hand. Chorb remembered that she whom he never named liked to take rides in cabs.

In a lane at the corner of the municipal opera house there was an old three-storied hotel of a disreputable type with rooms that were let by the week, or by the hour. Its black paint had peeled off in geographical patterns; ragged lace curtained its bleary windows; its inconspicuous front door was never locked. A pale but jaunty lackey led Chorb down a crooked corridor reeking of dampness and boiled cabbage into a room which Chorb recognized—by the picture of a pink *baigneuse* in a gilt frame over the bed—as the very one in which he and his wife had spent their first night together. Everything amused her then—the fat man in his shirt sleeves who was vomiting right in the passage, and the fact of their having chosen by chance such a beastly hotel, and the presence of a lovely blond hair in the wash

[62]

basin; but what tickled her most was the way they had escaped from her house. Immediately upon coming home from church she ran up to her room to change, while downstairs the guests were gathering for supper. Her father, in a dress coat of sturdy cloth, with a flabby grin on his apish face, clapped this or that man on the shoulder and served ponies of brandy himself. Her mother, in the meantime, led her closest friends, two by two, to inspect the bedroom meant for the young couple: with tender emotion, whispering under her breath, she pointed out the colossal eiderdown, the orange blossoms, the two pairs of brand-new bedroom slippers—large checkered ones, and tiny red ones with pompons—that she had aligned on the bedside rug, across which a Gothic inscription ran: *"We are together unto the tomb."* Presently, everybody moved toward the *hors d'œuvres*—and Chorb and his wife, after the briefest of consultations, fled through the back door, and only on the following morning, half an hour before the express train was to leave, reappeared to collect their luggage. Frau Keller had sobbed all night; her husband, who had always regarded Chorb (destitute Russian émigré and *littérateur*) with suspicion, now cursed his daughter's choice, the cost of the liquor, the local police that could do nothing. And several times, after the Chorbs had gone, the old man went to look at the hotel in the lane behind the opera house, and henceforward that black, purblind house became an object of disgust and attraction to him like the recollection of a crime.

While the trunk was being brought in, Chorb kept staring at the rosy chromo. When the door closed, he bent over the trunk and unlocked it. In a corner of the room, behind a loose strip of wallpaper, a mouse made a scuffing noise and then raced like a toy on rollers. Chorb turned on his heel with a start. The light bulb hanging from the ceiling on a cord swayed ever so gently, and the shadow of the cord glided across the green couch and broke at its edge. It was on that couch that he had slept on his nuptial night. She, on the regular bed, could be heard breathing with the even rhythm of a child. That night he had kissed her once—on the hollow of the throat—that had been all in the way of love-making.

The mouse was busy again. There exist small sounds that are more frightening than gunfire. Chorb left the trunk alone and paced the room a couple of times. A moth struck the lamp with a ping. Chorb wrenched the door open and went out.

On the way downstairs he realized how weary he was, and when he found himself in the alley the blurry blue of the May night made him dizzy. Upon turning into the boulevard he walked faster. A square. A stone *Herzog*. The black masses of the City Park. Chestnut trees now were in flower. *Then*, it had been autumn. He had gone for a long stroll with her on the eve of the wedding. How good was the earthy, damp, somewhat violety smell of the dead leaves strewing the sidewalk! On those enchanting overcast days the sky would be of a dull white, and the small twig-reflecting puddle in the middle of the black pavement resembled an insufficiently developed photograph. The gray-stone villas were separated by the mellow and motionless foliage of yellowing trees, and in front of the Kellers' house the leaves of a withering poplar had acquired the tone of transparent grapes. One glimpsed, too, a few birches behind the bars of the gate; ivy solidly muffed some of their boles, and Chorb made a point of telling her that ivy never grew on birches in Russia, and she remarked that the foxy tints of their minute leaves reminded her of spots of tender rust upon ironed linen. Oaks and chestnuts lined the sidewalk; their black bark was velveted with green rot; every now and then a leaf broke away to fly athwart the street like a scrap of wrapping paper. She attempted to catch it on the wing by means of a child's spade found near a heap of pink bricks at a spot where the street was under repair. A little way off the funnel of a workers' van emitted gray-blue smoke which drifted aslant and dissolved between the branches—and a resting workman, one hand on his hip, contemplated the young lady, as light as a dead leaf, dancing about with that little spade in her raised hand. She skipped, she laughed. Chorb, hunching his back a bit, walked behind her—and it seemed to him that happiness itself had that smell, the smell of dead leaves.

At present he hardly recognized the street, encumbered as it was with the nocturnal opulence of chestnut trees. A streetlamp glinted in front; over the glass a branch drooped, and several leaves at its end, saturated with light, were quite translucent. He came nearer. The shadow of the wicket, its checkerwork all distorted, swept up toward him from the sidewalk to entangle his feet. Beyond the gate, and beyond a dim gravel walk, loomed the front of the familiar house, dark except for the light in one open window. Within that amber chasm the housemaid was in the act of spreading with an ample sweep of her arms a snow-bright sheet on a bed. Loudly and curtly Chorb called out to her. With one hand he still gripped the wicket and the dewy touch of iron against his palm was the keenest of all memories.

The maid was already hurrying toward him. As she was to tell Frau Keller later, what struck her first was the fact that Chorb remained standing silently on the sidewalk although she had unlocked the little gate at once. "He had no hat," she related, "and the light of the streetlamp fell on his forehead, and his forehead was all sweaty, and the hair was glued to it by the sweat. I told him master and mistress were at the theater. I asked him why he was alone. His eyes were blazing, their look terrified me, and he seemed not to have shaved for quite a time. He said softly: 'Tell them that she is ill.' I asked: 'Where are you staying?' He said: 'Same old place,' and then added: 'That does not matter. I'll call again in the morning.' I suggested he wait—but he didn't reply and went away."

Thus Chorb traveled back to the very source of his recollections, an agonizing and yet blissful test now drawing to a close. All there remained was but a single night to be spent in that first chamber of their marriage, and by tomorrow the test would be passed and her image made perfect.

But as he trudged back to the hotel, up the boulevard, where on all the benches in the blue darkness sat hazy figures, Chorb suddenly understood that, despite exhaustion, he would not be able to sleep alone in that room with its naked bulb and whispery crannies. He reached the square and plodded along the city's main avenue—and now he knew what must be done. His quest, however, lasted a long while: This was a quiet and chaste town, and the secret by-street where one could buy love was unknown to Chorb. Only after an hour of helpless wandering, which caused his ears to sing and his feet to burn, did he enter that little lane—whereupon he accosted at once the first girl who hailed him.

"The night," said Chorb, scarcely unclenching his teeth.

The girl cocked her head, swung her handbag, and replied: "Twenty-five."

He nodded. Only much later, having glanced at her casually, Chorb noted with indifference that she was pretty enough, though considerably jaded, and that her bobbed hair was blond.

She had been in that hotel several times before, with other customers, and the wan, sharp-nosed lackey, who was tripping down as they were going upstairs gave her an amiable wink. While Chorb and she walked along the corridor, they could hear, from behind one of the doors, a bed creaking, rhythmically and weightily, as if a log was being sawed in two. A few doors further the same monotonous creak came from another room and as they passed by the girl looked back at Chorb with an expression of cold playfulness.

In silence he ushered her into his room—and immediately, with a profound anticipation of sleep, started to tear off his collar from its stud. The girl came up very close to him:

"And what about a small present?" she suggested, smiling.

Dreamily, absentmindedly, Chorb considered her, as he slowly grasped what she meant.

Upon receiving the banknotes, she carefully arranged them in her bag, uttered a light little sigh, and again rubbed herself against him.

"Shall I undress?" she asked with a shake of her bob.

"Yes, go to bed," muttered Chorb. "I'll give you some more in the morning."

The girl began to undo hastily the buttons of her blouse, and kept glancing at him askance, being slightly taken aback by his abstraction and gloom. He shed his clothes quickly and carelessly, got into the bed and turned to the wall.

"This fellow likes kinky stuff," vaguely conjectured the girl. With slow hands she folded her chemise, placed it upon a chair. Chorb was already fast asleep.

The girl wandered around the room. She noticed that the lid of the trunk standing by the window was slightly ajar; by squatting on her heels, she managed to peep under the lid's edge. Blinking and cautiously stretching out her bare arm, she palpated a woman's dress, a stocking, scraps of silk—all this stuffed in anyhow and smelling so nice that it made her feel sad.

Presently she straightened up, yawned, scratched her thigh, and just as she was, naked, but in her stockings, drew aside the window curtain. Behind the curtain the casement was open and one could make out, in the velvety depths, a corner of the opera house, the black shoulder of a stone Orpheus outlined against the blue of the night and a row of light along the dim façade which slanted off into darkness. Down there, far away, diminutive dark silhouettes swarmed as they emerged from bright doorways onto the semi-circular layers of illumined porch steps, to which glided up cars with shimmering headlights and smooth glistening tops. Only when the breakup was over and the brightness gone, the girl closed the curtain again. She switched off the light and stretched on the bed beside Chorb. Just before falling asleep she caught herself thinking that once or twice she had already been in that room: she remembered the pink picture on its wall.

Her sleep lasted not more than an hour: a ghastly deep-drawn howl roused her. It was Chorb screaming. He had woken up some time after midnight, had turned on his side and had seen his wife lying beside him. He screamed horribly, with visceral force. The white specter of a woman sprang off the bed. When, trembling, she turned on the light, Chorb was sitting among the tumbled bedclothes, his back to the wall, and through his spread fingers one eye could be seen burning with a mad flame. Then he slowly uncovered his face, slowly recognized the girl. With a frightened mutter she was hastily putting on her chemise.

And Chorb heaved a sigh of relief for he realized that the ordeal was over. He moved onto the green couch, and sat there, clasping his hairy shins and with a meaningless smile contemplating the harlot. That smile increased her terror; she turned away, did up one last hook, laced her boots, busied herself with the putting on of her hat.

At this moment the sound of voices and footsteps came from the corridor.

One could hear the voice of the lackey repeating mournfully: "But look here, there's a lady with him." And an irate guttural voice kept insisting: "But I'm telling you she's my daughter."

The footsteps stopped at the door. A knock followed.

The girl snatched her bag from the table and resolutely flung the door open. In front of her stood an amazed old gentleman in a lusterless top hat, a pearl stud gleaming in his starched shirt. From over his shoulder peered the tear-stained face of a stout lady with a veil on her hair. Behind them the puny pale lackey strained up on tiptoe, making big eyes and gesturing invitingly. The girl understood his signs and shot out into the corridor, past the old man, who turned his head in her wake with the same puzzled look and then crossed the threshold with his companion. The door closed. The girl and the lackey remained in the corridor. They exchanged a frightened glance and bent their heads to listen. But in the room all was silence. It seemed incredible that inside there should be three people. Not a single sound came from there.

"They don't speak," whispered the lackey and put his finger to his lips.

THE PASSENGER

Passazhir *was written early 1927 in Berlin, published in the* Rul', *Berlin, March 6, 1927, and included in the collection* Vozvrashchenie Chorba, *by V. Sirin, Slovo, Berlin, 1930. An English translation by Gleb Struve appeared in* Lovat Dickson's Magazine, *edited by P. Gilchrist Thompson (with my name on the cover reading V. Nobokov [sic]-Sirin), Vol. 2, No. 6, London, June 1934. It was reprinted in* A Century of Russian Prose and Verse from Pushkin to Nabokov, *edited by O. R. and R. P. Hughes and G. Struve, with the original* en regard, *New York, Harcourt, Brace, 1967. I was unable to use Struve's version in this volume for the same reasons that made me forgo his* "Tchorb's Return" *(see Introduction to it).*

The "writer" *in the story is not a self-portrait but the generalized image of a middle-brow author. The* "critic," *however, is a friendly sketch of a fellow émigré, Yuliy Ayhenvald, the well-known literary critic (1872–1928). Readers of the time recognized his precise, delicate little gestures and his fondness for playing with euphonically twinned phrases in his literary comments. By the end of the story everybody seems to have forgotten about the burnt match in the wineglass—something I would not have allowed to happen today.*

"Yes, Life is more talented than we," sighed the writer, tapping the cardboard mouthpiece of his Russian cigarette against the lid of his case. "The plots Life thinks up now and then! How can we compete with that goddess? Her works are untranslatable, undescribable."

"Copyright by the author," suggested the critic, smiling; he was a modest, myopic man with slim, restless fingers.

"Our last recourse, then, is to cheat," continued the writer, absentmindedly throwing a match into the critic's empty wineglass. "All that's left to us is to treat her creations as a film producer does a famous novel. The producer needs to prevent servant maids from being bored on Saturday nights; therefore he alters the novel beyond recognition; minces it, turns it inside out, throws out hundreds of episodes, introduces new characters and incidents he has invented himself—and all this for the sole purpose of having an entertaining film unfold without a hitch, punishing virtue in the beginning and vice at the end, a film perfectly natural in terms of its own conventions, and, above all, furnished with an unexpected but all-resolving outcome. Exactly thus do we, writers, alter the themes of Life to suit us in our drive toward some kind of conventional harmony, some kind of artistic conciseness. We spice our savorless plagiarisms with our own devices. We think that

Life's performance is too sweeping, too uneven, that her genius is too untidy. To indulge our readers we cut out of Life's untrammeled novels our neat little tales for the use of schoolchildren. Allow me, in this connection, to impart to you the following experience.

"I happened to be traveling in the sleeping car of an express. I love the process of settling into viatic quarters—the cool linen of the berth, the slow passage of the station's departing lights as they start moving behind the black windowpane. I remember how pleased I was that there was nobody in the bunk above me. I undressed, I lay down supine with my hands clasped under my head, and the lightness of the scant regulation blanket was a treat in comparison to the puffiness of hotel featherbeds. After some private musings—at the time I was anxious to write a story about the life of railway-car cleaning women—I put out the light and was soon asleep. And here let me use a device cropping up with dreary frequency in the sort of story to which mine promises to belong. Here it is—that old device which you must know so well: 'In the middle of the night I woke up suddenly.' What follows, however, is something less stale. I woke up and saw a foot."

"Excuse me, a what?" interrupted the modest critic, leaning forward and lifting his finger.

"I saw a foot," repeated the writer. "The compartment was now lighted. The train stood at a station. It was a man's foot, a foot of considerable size, in a coarse sock, through which the bluish toenail had worked a hole. It was planted solidly on a step of the bed ladder close to my face, and its owner, concealed from my sight by the upper bunk roofing me, was just on the point of making a last effort to hoist himself onto his ledge. I had ample time to inspect that foot in its gray, black-checkered sock and also part of the leg:

the violet vee of the garter on the side of the stout calf and its little hairs nastily sticking out through the mesh of the long underwear. It was altogether a most repellent limb. While I looked, it tensed, the tenacious big toe moved once or twice; then, finally, the whole extremity vigorously pushed off and soared out of sight. From above, came grunting and snuffling sounds leading one to conclude that the man was preparing to sleep. The light went out, and a few moments later the train jerked into motion.

"I don't know how to explain it to you, but that limb anguished me most oppressively. A resilient varicolored reptile. I found it disturbing that all I knew of the man was that evil-looking leg. His figure, his face, I never saw. His berth, which formed a low, dark ceiling over me, now seemed to have come lower; I almost felt its weight. No matter how hard I tried to imagine the aspect of my nocturnal fellow traveler all I could visualize was that conspicuous toenail which showed its bluish mother-of-pearl sheen through a hole in the wool of the sock. It may seem strange, in a general way, that such trifles should bother me but, per contra, is not every writer precisely a person who bothers about trifles? Anyhow, sleep did not come. I kept listening—had my unknown companion started to snore? Apparently he was not snoring but moaning. Of course, the knocking of train wheels at night is known to encourage aural hallucinations; yet I could not get over the impression that from up there, above me, came sounds of an unusual nature. I raised myself on one elbow. The sounds grew more distinct. The man on the upper berth was sobbing."

"What's that?" interrupted the critic. "Sobbing? I see. Sorry—didn't quite catch what you said." And, again dropping his hands in his lap and inclining his head to one side, the critic went on listening to the narrator.

"Yes, he was sobbing, and his sobs were atrocious. They choked him; he would noisily let his breath out as if having drunk at one gulp a quart of water, whereupon there followed rapid spasms of weeping with the mouth shut—the frightful parody of a cackle—and again he would draw in air and again let it out in short expirations of sobbing, with his mouth now open—to judge by the hah-hahing note. And all this against the shaky background of hammering wheels, which by this token became something like a moving stairway along which his sobs went up and came down. I lay motionless and listened—and felt, incidentally, that my face in the dark looked awfully silly, for it is always embarrassing to hear a stranger sobbing. And mind you, I was helplessly shackled to him by the fact of our sharing the same two-berth compartment, in the same unconcernedly rushing train. And he did not stop weeping; those dreadful arduous sobs kept up with me: we both—I below, the listener, and he overhead, the weeping one—sped sideways into night's remoteness at eighty kilometers an hour, and only a railway crash could have cleft our involuntary link.

"After a while he seemed to stop crying, but no sooner was I about to drop off than his sobs started to swell again and I even seemed to hear unintelligible words which he uttered in a kind of sepulchral, belly-deep voice between convulsive sighs. He was silent again, only snuffling a bit, and I lay with my eyes closed and saw in fancy his disgusting foot in its checkered sock. Somehow or other I managed to fall asleep; and at half past five the conductor wrenched the door open to call me. Sitting on my bed—and knocking my head every minute against the edge of the upper berth—I hurried to dress. Before going out with my bags into the corridor, I turned to look up at the upper berth, but the man was lying with his back to me, and had covered his head with his blanket. It was morning in the corridor, the sun had just risen, the fresh, blue shadow of the train ran over the grass, over the shrubs, swept sinuously up the slopes, rippled across the trunks of flickering birches—and an oblong pondlet shone dazzlingly in the middle of a field, then narrowed, dwindled to a silvery slit, and with a rapid clatter a cottage scuttled by, the tail of a road whisked under a crossing gate—and once more the numberless birches dizzied one with their flickering, sun-flecked palisade.

"The only other people in the corridor were two women with sleepy, sloppily made-up faces, and a little old man wearing suede gloves and a traveling cap. I detest rising early: for me the most ravishing dawn in the world cannot replace the hours of delicious morning sleep; and therefore I limited myself to a grumpy nod when the old gentleman asked me if I, too, was getting off at . . . he mentioned a big town where we were due in ten or fifteen minutes.

"The birches suddenly dispersed, half-a-dozen small houses poured down a hill, some of them, in their haste, barely missing being run over by the train; then a huge purple-red factory strode by flashing its windowpanes; somebody's chocolate hailed us from a ten-yard poster; another factory followed with its bright glass and chimneys; in short, there happened what usually happens when one is nearing a city. But all at once, to our surprise, the train braked convulsively and pulled up at a desolate whistle-stop, where an express had seemingly no business to dawdle. I also found it surprising that several policemen stood out there on the platform. I lowered a window and leaned out. 'Shut it, please,' said one of the men politely. The passengers in the corridor displayed some agitation.

A conductor passed and I asked what was the matter. 'There's a criminal on the train,' he replied and briefly explained that in the town at which we had stopped in the middle of the night, a murder had occurred on the eve: a betrayed husband had shot his wife and her lover. The ladies exclaimed '*ach!*', the old gentleman shook his head. Two policemen and a rosy-cheeked, plump, bowler-hatted detective who looked like a bookmaker entered the corridor. I was asked to go back to my berth. The policemen remained in the corridor, while the detective visited one compartment after another. I showed him my passport. His reddish-brown eyes glided over my face; he returned my passport. We stood, he and I, in that narrow coupé on the upper bunk of which slept a dark-cocooned figure. 'You may leave,' said the detective and stretched his arm toward that upper darkness: 'Papers, please.' The blanketed man kept on snoring. As I lingered in the doorway, I still heard that snoring and seemed to make out through it the sibilant echoes of his nocturnal sobs. 'Please, wake up,' said the detective, raising his voice; and with a kind of professional jerk he pulled at the edge of the blanket at the sleeper's nape. The latter stirred but continued to snore. The detective shook him by the shoulder. This was rather sickening. I turned away and stared at the window across the corridor, but did not really see it, while listening with my whole being to what was happening in the compartment.

"And imagine, I heard absolutely nothing out of the ordinary. The man on the upper berth sleepily mumbled something, the detective distinctly demanded his passport, distinctly thanked him, then went out and entered another compartment. That is all. But think only how nice it would have seemed—from the writer's viewpoint, naturally—if the evil-footed, weeping passenger had turned out to be a murderer, how nicely his tears in the night could have been explained, and, what is more, how nicely all that would have fitted into the frame of my night journey, the frame of a short story. Yet, it would appear that the plan of the Author, the plan of Life, was in this case, as in all others, a hundred times nicer."

The writer sighed and fell silent, as he sucked his cigarette, which had gone out long ago and was now all chewed up and damp with saliva. The critic was gazing at him with kindly eyes.

"Confess," spoke the writer again, "that beginning with the moment when I mentioned the police and the unscheduled stop, you were sure my sobbing passenger was a criminal?"

"I know your manner," said the critic, touching his interlocutor's shoulder with the tips of his fingers and in a gesture peculiar to him, instantly snatching back his hand. "If you were writing a detective story, your villain would have turned out to be not the person whom none of the characters suspect but the person whom everybody in the story suspects from the very beginning, thus fooling the experienced reader who is used to solutions proving to be *not* the obvious ones. I am well aware that you like to produce an impression of inexpectancy by means of the most natural denouement; but don't get carried away by your own method. There is much in life that is casual, and there is also much that is unusual. The Word is given the sublime right to enhance chance and to make of the transcendental something that is not accidental. Out of the present case, out of the dance of chance, you could have created a well-rounded story if you had transformed your fellow traveler into a murderer."

The writer sighed again.

"Yes, yes, that did occur to me. I might have added several details. I would have alluded to the passionate love he had for his wife. All kinds of inventions are possible. The trouble is that we are in the dark—maybe Life had in mind something totally different, something much more subtle and deep. The trouble is that I did not learn, and shall never learn, why the passenger cried."

"I intercede for the Word," gently said the critic. "You, as a writer of fiction, would have at least thought up some brilliant solution: your character was crying, perhaps, because he had lost his wallet at the station. I once knew someone, a grown-up man of martial appearance, who would weep or rather bawl when he had a toothache. No, thanks, no—don't pour me any more. That's sufficient, that's quite sufficient."

A LETTER THAT
NEVER REACHED
RUSSIA

Sometime in 1924, in émigré Berlin, I had begun a novel tentatively entitled "Happiness" (Schastie), some important elements of which were to be reslanted in Mashen'ka, *written in the spring of 1925 (published by* Slovo, *Berlin in 1925, translated into English under the title of* Mary *in 1970, McGraw-Hill, New York, and reprinted in Russian from the original text, by "Ardis" and McGraw-Hill, in 1974). Around Christmas 1924, I had two chapters of* Schastie *ready but then, for some forgotten but no doubt excellent reason, I scrapped Chapter One and most of Two. What I kept was a fragment representing a letter written in Berlin to my heroine who had remained in Russia. This appeared in* Rul' *(Berlin, January 29, 1925) as* Pis'mo *(Letter)* v Rossiyu, *and was collected in* Vozvrashchenie Chorba, *in Berlin, 1930. A literal rendering of the title would have been ambiguous and therefore had to be changed.*

My charming, dear, distant one, I presume you cannot have forgotten anything in the more than eight years of our separation, if you manage to remember even the gray-haired, azure-liveried watchman who did not bother us in the least when we would meet, skipping school, on a frosty Petersburg morning, in the Suvorov museum, so dusty, so small, so similar to a glorified snuffbox. How ardently we kissed behind a waxen grenadier's back! And later, when we came out of that antique dust, how dazzled we were by the silvery blaze of the Tavricheski Park, and how odd it was to hear the cheery, avid, deep-fetched grunts of soldiers, lunging on command, slithering across the icy ground, plunging a bayonet into the straw-bellied German-helmeted dummy in the middle of a Petersburg street.

Yes, I know that I had sworn, in my previous letter to you, not to mention the past, especially the trifles in our shared past; for we authors in exile are supposed to possess a lofty pudicity of expression, and yet, here I am, from the very first lines, disdaining that right to sublime imperfection, and deafening with epithets the recollection on which you touched with such lightness and grace. Not of the past, my love, do I wish to speak to you.

It is night. At night one perceives with a special intensity the immobility of objects—the lamp, the furniture, the framed photographs on one's desk. Now and then the water gulps and gurgles in its hidden pipes as if sobs were rising to the throat of the house. At night I go out for a stroll. Reflections of streetlamps trickle across the damp Berlin asphalt whose surface resembles a film of black grease with puddles nestling in its wrinkles. Here and there a garnet-red light glows over a fire-alarm box. A glass column, full of liquid yellow light, stands at the streetcar stop, and, for some reason, I get such a blissful, melancholy sensation when, late at night, its wheels screeching around the bend, a tram hurtles past, empty. Through its windows one can clearly see the rows of brightly lit brown seats between which a lone ticket collector with a black satchel at his side makes his way, reeling a bit and thus looking a little tight—as he moves against the direction of the car's travel.

As I wander along some silent, dark street, I like to hear a man coming home. The man himself is not visible in the darkness, and you never know beforehand which front door will come alive to accept a key with grinding condescension, swing open, pause, retained by the counterweight, slam shut; the key will grind again from the inside, and, in the depths beyond the glass pane of the door, a soft radiance will linger for one marvelous minute.

A car rolls by on pillars of wet light. It is black, with a yellow stripe beneath the windows. It trumpets gruffly into the ear of the night, and its shadow passes under my feet. By now the street is totally deserted—except for an aged great Dane whose claws rap on the sidewalk as it reluctantly takes for a walk a listless, pretty, hatless girl with an opened umbrella. When she passes under the garnet bulb (on her left, above the fire alarm), a single taut, black segment of her umbrella reddens damply.

[84]

And beyond the bend, above the sidewalk—how unexpectedly!—the front of a cinema ripples in diamonds. Inside, on its rectangular, moon-pale screen you can watch more-or-less skillfully trained mimes: the huge face of a girl with gray, shimmering eyes and black lips traversed vertically by glistening cracks, approaches from the screen, keeps growing as it gazes into the dark hall, and a wonderful, long, shining tear runs down one cheek. And occasionally (a heavenly moment!) there appears real life, unaware that it is being filmed: a chance crowd, bright waters, a noiselessly but visibly rustling tree.

Further on, at the corner of a square, a stout prostitute in black furs slowly walks to and fro, stopping occasionally in front of a harshly lighted shop window where a rouged woman of wax shows off to night wanderers her streamy, emerald gown and the shiny silk of her peach-colored stockings. I like to observe this placid middle-aged whore, as she is approached by an elderly man with a mustache, who came on business that morning from Papenburg (first he passes her and takes two backward glances). She will conduct him unhurriedly to a room in a nearby building, which, in the daytime, is quite undistinguishable from other, equally ordinary buildings. A polite and impassive old porter keeps an all-night vigil in the unlighted front hall. At the top of a steep staircase an equally impassive old woman will unlock with sage unconcern an unoccupied room and receive payment for it.

And do you know with what a marvelous clatter the brightly lit train, all its windows laughing, sweeps across the bridge above the street! Probably it goes no further than the suburbs, but in that instant the darkness beneath the black span of the bridge is filled with such mighty metallic music that I cannot help imagining the sunny lands toward which I shall depart as soon as I have procured those extra hundred marks for which I long so blandly, so lightheartedly.

I am so lighthearted that sometimes I even enjoy watching people dancing in the local café. Many fellow exiles of mine denounce indignantly (and in this indignation there is a pinch of pleasure) fashionable abominations, including current dances. But fashion is a creature of man's mediocrity, a certain level of life, the vulgarity of equality, and to denounce it means admitting that mediocrity can create something (whether it be a form of government or a new kind of hairdo) worth making a fuss about. And of course these so-called modern dances of ours are actually anything but modern: the craze goes back to the days of the Directoire, for then as now women's dresses were worn next to the skin, and the musicians were Negroes. Fashion breathes through the centuries: the dome-shaped crinoline of the middle 1800s was the full inhalation of fashion's breath, followed by exhalation: narrowing skirts, close dances. Our dances, after all, are very natural and pretty innocent, and sometimes—in London ballrooms—perfectly graceful in their monotony. We all remember what Pushkin wrote about the waltz: "monotonous and mad." It's all the same thing. As for the deterioration of morals...Here's what I found in D'Agricourt's memoirs: "I know nothing more depraved than the minuet, which they see fit to dance in our cities."

And so I enjoy watching, in the *café dansants* here, how "pair after pair flick by," to quote Pushkin again. Amusingly made-up eyes sparkle with simple human merriment. Black-trousered and light-stockinged legs touch. Feet turn this way and that. And meanwhile, outside the door, waits my faithful, my lonely night with its moist reflections, hooting cars, and gusts of high-blowing wind.

On that kind of night, at the Russian Orthodox cemetery far outside the city, an old lady of seventy committed suicide on the grave of her recently deceased husband. I happened to go there the next morning, and the watchman, a badly crippled veteran of the Denikin campaign, moving on crutches that creaked with every swing of his body, showed me the white cross on which she hanged herself, and the yellow strands still adhering where the rope ("brand-new one," he said gently) had chafed. Most mysterious and enchanting of all, though, were the crescent-shaped prints left by her heels, tiny as a child's, on the damp soil by the plinth. "She trampled the ground a bit, poor thing, but apart from that there's no mess at all," observed the watchman calmly, and, glancing at those yellow strands and at those little depressions, I suddenly realized that one can distinguish a naive smile even in death. Possibly, dear, my main reason for writing this letter is to tell you of that easy, gentle end. Thus the Berlin night resolved itself.

Listen: I am ideally happy. My happiness is a kind of challenge. As I wander along the streets and the squares and the paths by the canal, absently sensing the lips of dampness through my worn soles, I carry proudly my ineffable happiness. The centuries will roll by, and schoolboys will yawn over the history of our upheavals; everything will pass, but my happiness, dear, my happiness will remain, in the moist reflection of a streetlamp, in the cautious bend of stone steps that descend into the canal's black waters, in the smiles of a dancing couple, in everything with which God so generously surrounds human loneliness.

A GUIDE
TO BERLIN

Written in December 1925 in Berlin, Putevoditel' po Berlinu *was published in the* Rul', *December 24, 1925, and collected in* Vozvrashchenie Chorba, Slovo, *Berlin, 1930.*

Despite its simple appearance this Guide *is one of my trickiest pieces. Its translation has caused my son and me a tremendous amount of healthy trouble. Two or three scattered phrases have been added for the sake of factual clarity.*

.

In the morning I visited the Zoo and now I am entering a pub with my friend and usual pot companion. Its sky-blue sign bears a white inscription, *Löwenbräu*, accompanied by the portrait of a lion with a winking eye and mug of beer. We sit down and I start telling my friend about utility pipes, streetcars, and other important matters.

1 The Pipes

In front of the house where I live a gigantic black pipe lies along the outer edge of the sidewalk. A couple of feet away, in the same file, lies another, then a third and a fourth —the street's iron entrails, still idle, not yet lowered into the ground, deep under the asphalt. For the first few days after they were unloaded, with a hollow clanging, from trucks, little boys would run on them up and down and crawl on all fours through those round tunnels, but a week later nobody was playing any more and thick snow was falling instead; and now, when, cautiously probing the treacherous glaze of the sidewalk with my thick rubberheeled stick, I go out in the flat gray light of early morning, an even stripe of fresh snow stretches along the upper side of each black pipe while up the interior slope at the very mouth of the pipe which is nearest to the turn of the tracks, the reflection of a still illumined tram sweeps up like bright-orange heat lightning. Today someone wrote "Otto" with his finger on the strip of virgin snow and I thought how beautifully that name, with its two soft o's flanking the pair of gentle consonants, suited the silent layer of snow upon that pipe with its two orifices and its tacit tunnel.

2 The Streetcar

The streetcar will vanish in twenty years or so, just as the horse-drawn tram has vanished. Already I feel it has an air of antiquity, a kind of old-fashioned charm. Everything about it is a little clumsy and rickety and if a curve is taken a little too fast, and the trolley pole jumps the wire, and the conductor, or even one of the passengers, leans out over the car's stern, looks up, and jiggles the cord until the pole is back in place, I always think that the coach driver of old must sometimes have dropped his whip, reined in his four-horse team, sent after it the lad in long-skirted livery who sat beside him on the box and gave piercing blasts on his horn while, clattering over the cobblestones, the coach swung through a village.

The conductor who gives out tickets has very unusual hands. They work as nimbly as those of a pianist, but, instead of being limp, sweaty and soft-nailed, the ticketman's hands are so coarse that when you are pouring change into his palm and happen to touch that palm which seems to have developed a harsh chitinous crust, you feel a kind of moral discomfort. They are extraordinarily agile and efficient hands, despite their roughness and the thickness of the fingers. I watch him with curiosity as he clamps the ticket with his broad black fingernail and punches it in two places, rummages in his leather purse, scoops up coins to make change, immediately slaps the purse shut, and yanks the bell cord, or, with a shove of his thumb, throws open the special little window in the forward door to hand tickets to people on the front platform. And all the time the car sways, passengers standing in the aisle grab at the overhead straps, and surge back and forth—but he will not drop a single coin or a single ticket torn from his roll. In these winter days the bottom half of the forward door is curtained with green cloth, the windows are clouded with frost, Christmas trees for sale throng the edge of the sidewalk at each stop, the passengers' feet are numb with cold, and sometimes a gray worsted mitten clothes the conductor's hand. At the end of the line the front car uncouples, enters a siding, runs around the remaining one and approaches it from behind. There is something reminiscent of a submissive female in the way the second car waits as the first, male, trolley, sending up a small crackling flame, rolls up and couples on. And (minus the biological metaphor) I am reminded of how, some eighteen years ago in Petersburg, the horses used to be unhitched and led around the potbellied blue tram.

The horse-drawn tram has vanished, and so will the trolley, and some eccentric Berlin writer in the twenties of the twenty-first century, wishing to portray our time, will go to a museum of technological history and locate a hundred-year-old streetcar, yellow, uncouth, with old-fashioned curved seats, and in a museum of old costumes dig up a black, shiny-buttoned conductor's uniform. Then he will go home and compile a description of Berlin streets in bygone days. Everything, every trifle, will be valuable and meaningful: the conductor's purse, the advertisement over the window, that peculiar jolting motion which our great-grandchildren will perhaps imagine—everything will be ennobled and justified by its age.

I think that here lies the sense of literary creation: to portray ordinary objects as they will be reflected in the kindly mirrors of future times; to find in the objects around us the fragrant tenderness that only posterity will discern and appreciate in the far-off times when every trifle of our plain everyday life will become exquisite and festive in its own right: the times when a man who might put on the most ordinary jacket of today will be dressed up for an elegant masquerade.

3 Work

Here are examples of various kinds of work that I observe from the crammed tram in which a compassionate woman can always be relied upon to cede me her window seat— while trying not to look too closely at me.

At an intersection the pavement has been torn up next to the track; by turns, four workmen are pounding an iron stake with mallets; the first one strikes, and the second is already lowering his mallet with a sweeping, accurate swing; the second mallet crashes down and is rising sky-ward as the third and then the fourth bang down in rhythmical succession. I listen to their unhurried clanging, like four repeated notes of an iron carillon.

A young white-capped baker flashes by on his tricycle; there is something angelic about a lad dusted with flour. A van jingles past with cases on its roof containing rows of emerald-glittering empty bottles, collected from taverns. A long, black larch tree mysteriously travels by in a cart. The tree lies flat; its tip quivers gently, while the earth-covered roots, enveloped in sturdy burlap, form an enormous beige bomblike sphere at its base. A postman, who has placed the mouth of a sack under a cobalt-colored mailbox, fastens it on from below, and secretly, invisibly, with a hurried rustling, the box empties and the postman claps shut the square jaws of the bag, now grown full and heavy. But perhaps fairest of all are the carcasses, chrome yellow, with pink blotches, and arabesques, piled on a truck, and the man in apron and leather hood with a long neck flap who heaves each carcass onto his back and, hunched over, carries it across the sidewalk into the butcher's red shop.

4 Eden

Every large city has its own, man-made Eden on earth.

If churches speak to us of the Gospel, zoos remind us of the solemn, and tender, beginning of the Old Testament. The only sad part is that this artificial Eden is all behind bars, although it is also true that if there were no enclosures the very first dingo would savage me. It is Eden none the less, insofar as man is able to reproduce it, and it is with good reason that the large hotel across from the Berlin Zoo is named after that garden.

In the wintertime, when the tropical animals have been hidden away, I recommend visiting the amphibian, insect, and fish house. Rows of illuminated displays behind glass in the dimly lit hall resemble the portholes through which

Captain Nemo gazed out of his submarine at the sea creatures undulating among the ruins of Atlantis. Behind the glass, in bright recesses, transparent fishes glide with flashing fins, marine flowers breathe, and, on a patch of sand, lies a live, crimson five-pointed star. This, then, is where the notorious emblem originated—at the very bottom of the ocean, in the murk of sunken Atlantica, which long ago lived through various upheavals while pottering about topical utopias and other inanities that cripple us today.

Oh, do not omit to watch the giant tortoises being fed. These ponderous, ancient corneous cupolas were brought from the Galapagos Islands. With a decrepit kind of circumspection, a wrinkly flat head and two totally useless paws emerge in slow motion from under the two-hundred-pound dome. And with its thick, spongy tongue, suggesting somehow that of a cacological idiot slackly vomiting his monstrous speech, the turtle sticks its head into a heap of wet vegetables and messily munches their leaves.

But that dome above it—ah, that dome, that ageless, well-rubbed, dull bronze, that splendid burden of time....

5 The Pub

"That's a very poor guide," my usual pot companion says glumly. "Who cares about how you took a streetcar and went to the Berlin Aquarium?"

The pub in which he and I are sitting is divided into two parts, one large, the other somewhat smaller. A billiard table occupies the center of the former; there are a few tables in the corners; a bar faces the entrance, and bottles stand on shelves behind the bar. On the wall, between the windows, newspapers and magazines mounted on short staffs hang like paper banners. At the far end there is a wide passageway, through which one sees a cramped little room with a green couch under a mirror, out of which an oval table with a checked oilcloth topples and takes up its solid position in front of the couch. That room is part of the publican's humble little apartment. There his wife, with faded looks and big breasts, is feeding soup to a blond child.

"It's of no interest," my friend affirms with a mournful yawn. "What do trams and tortoises matter? And anyway the whole thing is simply a bore. A boring, foreign city, and expensive to live in, too...."

From our place near the bar one can make out very distinctly the couch, the mirror, and the table in the background beyond the passage. The woman is clearing the table. Propped on his elbows, the child attentively examines an illustrated magazine on its useless handle.

"What do you see down there?" asks my companion and turns slowly, with a sigh, and the chair creaks heavily under him.

There, under the mirror, the child still sits alone. But he is now looking our way. From there he can see the inside of the tavern—the green island of the billiard table, the ivory ball he is forbidden to touch, the metallic gloss of the bar, a pair of fat truckers at one table and the two of us at another. He has long since grown used to this scene and is not dismayed by its proximity. Yet there is one thing I know. Whatever happens to him in life, he will always remember the picture he saw every day of his childhood from the little room where he was fed his soup. He will remember the billiard table and the coatless evening visitor who used to draw back his sharp white elbow and hit the ball with his cue, and the blue-gray cigar smoke, and the din of voices, and my empty right sleeve and scarred face, and his father behind the bar, filling a mug for me from the tap.

"I can't understand what you see down there," says my friend, turning back toward me.

What indeed! How can I demonstrate to him that I have glimpsed somebody's future recollection?

THE DOORBELL

The reader will be sorry to learn that the exact date of the publication of this story has not been established. It certainly appeared in the Rul', *Berlin, probably in 1927, and was republished in the* Vozvrashchenie Chorba *collection,* Slovo, *Berlin, 1930.*

Seven years had passed since he and she had parted in Petersburg. God, what a crush there had been at the Nikolaevsky Station! Don't stand so close—the train is about to start. Well, here we go, good-bye, dearest.... She walked alongside, tall, thin, wearing a raincoat, with a black-and-white scarf around her neck, and a slow current carried her off backwards. A Red Army recruit, he took part, reluctantly and confusedly, in the Civil War. Then, one beautiful night, to the ecstatic stridulation of prairie crickets, he went over to the Whites. A year later, in 1920, not long before leaving Russia, on the steep, stony Chainaya Street in Yalta, he ran into his uncle, a Moscow lawyer. Why, yes, there was news—two letters. She was leaving for Germany and already had obtained a passport. You look fine, young man. And at last Russia let go of him—a permanent leave, according to some. Russia had held him for a long time; he had slowly slithered down from north to south, and Russia kept trying to keep him in her grasp, with the taking of Tver, Kharkov, Belgorod, and various interesting little villages, but it was no use. She had in store for him one last temptation, one last gift—the Crimea—but even that did not help. He left. And on board the ship he made the acquaintance of a young Englishman, a jolly chap and an athlete, who was on his way to Africa.

Nikolay visited Africa, and Italy, and for some reason the Canary Islands, and then Africa again, where he served for a while in the Foreign Legion. At first he recalled her often, then rarely, then again more and more often. Her second husband, the German industrialist Kind, died during the war. He had owned a goodish bit of real estate in Berlin, and Nikolay assumed there was no danger of her going hungry there. But how quickly time passed! Amazing! ... Had seven whole years really gone by?

During those years he had grown hardier, rougher, had lost an index finger, and had learned two languages—Italian and English. The color of his eyes had become lighter and their expression more candid owing to the smooth rustic tan that covered his face. He smoked a pipe. His walk, which had always had the solidity characteristic of short-legged people, now acquired a remarkable rhythm. One thing about him had not changed at all: his laugh, accompanied by a quip and a twinkle.

He had quite a time, chuckling softly and shaking his head, before he finally decided to drop everything and by easy stages make his way to Berlin. On one occasion—at a newsstand, somewhere in Italy, he noticed an émigré Russian paper, published in Berlin. He wrote to the paper to place an advertisement under Personal: so-and-so seeks so-and-so. He got no reply. On a side trip to Corsica, he met a fellow Russian, the old journalist Grushevski, who was leaving for Berlin. Make inquiries on my behalf. Perhaps you'll find her. Tell her I am alive and well.... But this source did not bring any news either. Now it was high time to take Berlin by storm. There, on the spot, the search would be simpler. He had a lot of trouble obtaining a German visa, and he was running out of funds. Oh, well, he would get there one way or another....

And so he did. Wearing a trenchcoat and a checked cap, short and broad-shouldered, with a pipe between his teeth and a battered valise in his good hand, he exited onto the square in front of the station. There he stopped to admire a great jewel-bright advertisement that inched its way through the darkness, then vanished and started again from another point. He spent a bad night in a stuffy room in a cheap hotel, trying to think of ways to begin the search. The address bureau, the office of the Russian-language newspaper . . . Seven years. She must really have aged. It was rotten of him to have waited so long; he could have come sooner. But ah those years, that stupendous roaming about the world, the obscure ill-paid jobs, chances taken and chucked, the excitement of freedom, the freedom he had dreamed of in childhood! . . . It was pure Jack London. . . . And here he was again: a new city, a suspiciously itchy featherbed, and the screech of a late tram. He groped for his matches, and with a habitual movement of his index stump began pressing the soft tobacco into the pipebowl.

When traveling the way he did you forget the names of time; they are crowded out by those of places. In the morning, when Nikolay went out intending to go to the police station, the gratings were down on all the shop fronts. It was a damned Sunday. So much for the address office and the newspaper. It was also late autumn: windy weather, asters in the public gardens, a sky of solid white, yellow trees, yellow trams, the nasal honking of rheumy taxis. A chill of excitement came over him at the idea that he was in the same town as she. A fifty-pfennig coin bought him a glass of port in a cab drivers' bar, and the wine on an empty stomach had a pleasant effect. Here and there in the streets there came a sprinkling of Russian speech: ". . . *Skol'ko raz ya tebe govorila* (how many times have I told you)." And again, after the passage of several natives: ". . . He's willing to sell them to me, but frankly, I . . ." The excitement made him chuckle and finish each pipeful much more quickly than usual. ". . . Seemed to be gone, but now Grisha's down with it too. . . ." He considered going up to the next pair of Russians and asking, very politely: "Do you know by any chance Olga Kind, born Countess Karski?" They must all know each other in this bit of provincial Russia gone astray.

It was already evening, and, in the twilight, a beautiful tangerine light had filled the glassed tiers of a huge department store when Nikolay noticed, on one of the sides of a front door, a small white sign that said: "I. S. Weiner, Dentist. From Petrograd." An unexpected recollection virtually scalded him. This fine friend of ours is pretty well decayed and must go. In the window, right in front of the torture seat, inset glass photographs displayed Swiss landscapes. . . . The window gave on Moika Street. Rinse, please. And Dr. Weiner, a fat, placid, white-gowned old man in perspicacious glasses, sorted his tinkling instruments. She used to go to him for treatment, and so did his cousins, and they even used to say to each other, when they quarreled for some reason or other, "How would you like a Weiner?" (i.e., a punch in the mouth?). Nikolay dallied in front of the door, on the point of ringing the bell, remembering it was Sunday; he thought some more and rang anyway. There was a buzzing in the lock and the door gave. He went up one flight. A maid opened the door. "No, the doctor is not receiving today." "My teeth are fine," objected Nikolay in very poor German. "Dr. Weiner is an old friend of mine. My name is Galatov—I'm sure he remembers me. . . ." "I'll tell him," said the maid.

A moment later a middle-aged man in a frogged velveteen jacket came out into the hallway. He had a carroty complexion and seemed extremely friendly. After a cheerful greeting he added in Russian. "I don't remember you, though—there must be a mistake." Nikolay looked at him and apologized: "Afraid so. I don't remember you either. I was expecting to find the Dr. Weiner who lived on Moika Street in Petersburg before the Revolution, but got the wrong one. Sorry."

"Oh, that must be a namesake of mine. A common namesake. I lived on Zagorodny Avenue."

"We all used to go to him," explained Nikolay, "and well, I thought... You see, I'm trying to locate a certain lady, a Madame Kind, that's the name of her second husband——"

Weiner bit his lip, looked away with an intent expression, then addressed him again. "Wait a minute.... I seem to recall... I seem to recall a Madame Kind who came to see me here not long ago and was also under the impression —— We'll know for sure in a minute. Be kind enough to step into my office."

The office remained a blur in Nikolay's vision. He did not take his eyes off Weiner's impeccable calvities as the latter bent over his appointment book.

"We'll know for sure in a minute," he repeated, running his fingers across the pages. "We'll know for sure in just a minute. We'll know in just... Here we are. Frau Kind. Gold filling and some other work—which I can't make out, there's a blot here."

"And what's the first name and patronymic?" asked Nikolay, approaching the table and almost knocking off an ashtray with his cuff.

"That's in the book too. Olga Kirillovna."

"Right," said Nikolay with a sigh of relief.

"The address is Plannerstrasse 59, care of Babb," said Weiner with a smack of his lips and rapidly copied the address on a separate slip. "Second street from here. Here you are. Very happy to be of service. Is she a relative of yours?"

"My mother," replied Nikolay.

Coming out of the dentist's, he proceeded with a somewhat quickened step. Finding her so easily astonished him like a card trick. He had never paused to think, while traveling to Berlin, that she might long since have died or moved to a different city, and yet the trick had worked. Weiner had turned out to be a different Weiner—and yet Fate found a way. Beautiful city, beautiful rain! (the pearly autumn drizzle seemed to fall in a whisper and the streets were dark). How would she greet him—tenderly? Sadly? Or with complete calm. She had not spoiled him as a child. You are forbidden to run through the drawing room while I am playing the piano. As he grew up, he would feel more and more frequently that she did not have much use for him. Now he tried to picture her face, but his thoughts obstinately refused to take on color, and he simply could not gather in a living optical image what he knew in his mind: her tall, thin figure with that loosely-assembled look about it; her dark hair with streaks of gray at the temples; her large, pale mouth; the old raincoat she had on the last time he saw her; and the tired, bitter expression of an aging woman, that seemed to have always been on her face—even before the death of his father, Admiral Galatov, who had shot himself shortly before the Revolution. Number fifty-one. Eight houses more.

He suddenly realized that he was unendurably, indecently perturbed, much more so than he had been, for example, that first time when he lay pressing his sweat-drenched body against the side of a cliff and aiming at an approaching whirlwind, a white scarecrow on a splendid Arabian horse. He stopped just short of No. 59, took out his pipe and a rubber tobacco pouch; stuffed the bowl slowly and carefully, without spilling a single shred; lit up, coddled the flame, drew, watched the fiery mound swell, gulped a mouthful of sweetish, tongue-prickling smoke, carefully expelled it, and with a firm, unhurried step walked up to the house.

The stairs were so dark that he stumbled a couple of times. When, in the dense blackness, he reached the second-floor landing, he struck a match and made out a gilt name plate. Wrong name. It was only much higher that he found the odd name "Babb." The flamelet burned his fingers and went out. God, my heart is pounding.... He groped for the bell in the dark and rang. Then he removed the pipe from between his teeth and began waiting, feeling an agonizing smile rend his mouth.

Then he heard a lock, a bolt make a double resonant sound, and the door, as if swung by a violent wind, burst open. It was just as dark in the anteroom as on the stairs, and out of that darkness floated a vibrant, joyful voice. "The lights are out in the whole building—*eto oozhas*, it's appalling"—and Nikolay recognized at once that long emphatic "oo" and on its basis instantly reconstructed down to the most minute feature the person who now stood, still concealed by darkness, in the doorway.

"Sure, can't see a thing," said he with a laugh and advanced toward her.

Her cry was as startled as if a strong hand had struck her. In the dark he found her arms, and shoulders, and bumped against something (probably the umbrella stand).

"No, no, it's not possible..." She kept repeating rapidly as she backed away.

"Hold still, Mother, hold still for a minute," he said, hitting something again (this time it was the half-open front door, which shut with a great slam).

"It can't be... Nicky, Nick——."

He was kissing her at random, on the cheeks, on the hair, everywhere, unable to see anything in the dark but with some interior vision recognizing all of her from head to toe, and only one thing about her had changed (and even this novelty unexpectedly made him recall his earliest childhood, when she used to play the piano): the strong, elegant smell of perfume—as if those intervening years had not existed, the years of his adolescence and her widowhood, when she no longer wore perfume and faded so sorrowfully —it seemed as if nothing of that had happened, and he had passed straight from distant exile into childhood.... "It's you. You've come. You're really here," she prattled, pressing her soft lips against him. "It's good.... This is how it should be...."

"Isn't there any light anywhere?" Nikolay inquired cheerfully.

She opened an inner door and said excitedly, "Yes, come on. I've lit some candles there."

"Well, let me look at you," he said, entering the flickering aura of candlelight and gazing avidly at his mother. Her dark hair had been bleached a very light strawlike shade.

"Well, don't you recognize me?" she asked, with a nervous intake of breath, then added hurriedly, "Don't stare at me like that. Come on, tell me all the news! What a tan you have... my goodness! Yes, tell me everything!"

That blond bob... And her face was made up with excruciating care. The moist streak of a tear, though, had eaten through the rosy paint, and her mascara-laden lashes were wet, and the powder on the wings of her nose had turned violet. She was wearing a glossy blue dress closed at the throat. And everything about her was unfamiliar, restless and frightening.

"You're probably expecting company, Mother," observed Nikolay, and not quite knowing what to say next, energetically threw off his overcoat.

She moved away from him toward the table, which was set for a meal and sparkled with crystal in the semidarkness; then she came back toward him, and mechanically glanced at herself in the shadow-blurred mirror.

"So many years have passed. . . . Goodness! I can hardly believe my eyes. Oh yes, I have friends coming tonight. I'll call them off. I'll phone them. I'll do something. I must call them off. . . . Oh Lord. . . ."

She pressed against him, palpating him to find out how real he was.

"Calm down, Mother, what's the matter with you—this is overdoing it. Let's sit down somewhere. *Comment vas-tu?* How does life treat you?" . . . And, for some reason fearing the answers to his questions, he started telling her about himself, in the snappy neat way he had, puffing on his pipe, trying to drown his astonishment in words and smoke. It turned out that, after all, she had seen his ad and had been in touch with the old journalist and been on the point of writing to Nikolay—always on the point. . . . Now that he had seen her face distorted by its make-up and her artificially fair hair he felt that her voice, too, was no longer the same. And as he described his adventures, without a moment's pause, he glanced around the half-lit, quiv-

[109]

ering room, at its awful middle-class trappings—the toy cat on the mantelpiece, the coy screen from behind which protruded the foot of the bed, the picture of Friedrich the Great playing the flute, the bookless shelf with the little vases in which the reflected lights darted up and down like mercury.... As his eyes roamed around he also inspected something he had previously only noticed in passing: that table—a table set for two, with liqueurs, a bottle of Asti, two tall wine glasses, and an enormous pink cake adorned with a ring of still unlit little candles. "... Of course, I immediately jumped out of my tent, and what do you think it turned out to be? Come on, guess!"

She seemed to emerge from a trance, and gave him a wild look (she was reclining next to him on the divan, her temples compressed between her hands, and her peach-colored stockings gave off an unfamiliar sheen).

"Aren't you listening, Mother?"

"Why, yes—I am...."

And now he noticed something else: she was oddly absent, as if she were listening not to his words but to a doomful thing coming from afar, menacing and inevitable. He went on with his jolly narrative, but then stopped again and asked, "That cake—in whose honor is it? Looks awfully good."

His mother responded with a flustered smile. "Oh, it's a little stunt. I told you I was expecting company."

"It reminded me awfully of Petersburg," said Nikolay. "Remember how you once made a mistake and forgot one candle? I had turned ten, but there were only nine candles. *Tu escamotas* my birthday. I bawled my head off. And how many do we have here?"

"Oh, what does it matter?" she shouted, and rose, almost as if she wanted to block his view of the table. "Why don't you tell me instead what time it is? I must ring up and cancel the party.... I must do something."

"Quarter past seven," said Nikolay.

"*Trop tard, trop tard!*" she raised her voice again. "All right! At this point it no longer matters...."

Both fell silent. She resumed her seat. Nikolay was trying to force himself to hug her, to cuddle up to her, to ask, "Listen, Mother—what has happened to you? Come on: out with it." He took another look at the brilliant table and counted the candles ringing the cake. There were twenty-five of them. Twenty-five! And he was already twenty-eight....

"Please don't examine my room like that!" said his mother. "You look like a regular detective! It's a horrid hole. I would gladly move elsewhere, but I sold the villa that Kind left me." Abruptly she gave a small gasp: "Wait a minute—what was that? Did you make that noise?"

"Yes," answered Nikolay. "I'm knocking the ashes out of my pipe. But tell me: you do still have enough money? You're not having any trouble making ends meet?"

She busied herself with readjusting a ribbon on her sleeve and spoke without looking at him: "Yes.... Of course. He left me a few foreign stocks, a hospital and an ancient prison. A prison! ... But I must warn you that I have barely enough to live on. For Heaven's sake stop knocking with that pipe. I must warn you that I ... That I cannot ... Oh, you understand, Nick—it would be hard for me to support you."

"What on earth are you talking about, Mother?" exclaimed Nikolay (and at that moment, like a stupid sun issuing from behind a stupid cloud, the electric light burst forth from the ceiling). "There, we can snuff out those tapers now; it was like squatting in the Mostaga Mausoleum.

You see, I do have a small supply of cash, and anyway, I like to be as free as a damned fowl of some sort.... Come, sit down—stop running around the room."

Tall, thin, bright blue, she stopped in front of him and now, in the full light, he saw how much she had aged, how insistently the wrinkles on her cheeks and forehead showed through the make-up. And that awful bleached hair! ...

"You came tumbling in so suddenly," she said and, biting her lips, she consulted a small clock standing on the shelf. "Like snow out of a cloudless sky.... It's fast. No, it's stopped. I'm having company tonight, and here you arrive. It's a crazy situation...."

"Nonsense, Mother. They'll come, they'll see your son has arrived, and very soon they'll evaporate. And before the evening's over you and I will go to some music hall, and have supper somewhere.... I remember seeing an African show—that was really something! Imagine—about fifty Negroes, and a rather large, the size of, say——"

The doorbell buzzed loudly in the front hall. Olga Kirillovna, who had perched on the arm of a chair, gave a start and straightened up.

"Wait, I'll get it," said Nikolay, rising.

She caught him by the sleeve. Her face was twitching. The bell stopped. The caller waited.

"It must be your guests," said Nikolay. "Your twenty-five guests. We have to let them in."

His mother gave a brusque shake of her head and resumed listening intently.

"It isn't right——" began Nikolay.

She pulled at his sleeve, whispering, "Don't you dare! I don't want to ... Don't you dare ..."

The bell started buzzing again, insistently and irritably this time. And it buzzed on for a long time.

"Let me go," said Nikolay. "This is silly. If somebody rings you have to answer the door. What are you frightened of?"

"Don't you dare—do you hear," she repeated, spasmodically clutching at his hand. "I implore you.... Nicky, Nicky, Nicky! ... Don't!"

The bell stopped. It was replaced by a series of vigorous knocks, produced, it seemed, by the stout knob of a cane.

Nikolay headed resolutely for the front hall. But before he reached it his mother had grabbed him by the shoulders, and tried with all her might to drag him back, whispering all the while, "Don't you dare.... Don't you dare.... For God's sake! ..."

The bell sounded again, briefly and angrily.

"It's your business," said Nikolay with a laugh and, thrusting his hands into his pockets, walked the length of the room. This is a real nightmare, he thought, and chuckled again.

The ringing had stopped. All was still. Apparently the ringer had got fed up and left. Nikolay went up to the table, contemplated the splendid cake with its bright frosting and twenty-five festive candles, and the two wine glasses. Nearby, as if hiding in the bottle's shadow, lay a small white cardboard box. He picked it up and took off the lid. It contained a brand-new, rather tasteless silver cigarette case.

"And that's that," said Nikolay.

His mother, who was half-reclining on the couch with her face buried in a cushion, was convulsed with sobs. In previous years he had often seen her cry, but then she had cried quite differently: while sitting at table, for instance, she would cry without turning her face away, and blow her nose loudly and talk, talk, talk; yet now she was weeping so girlishly, was lying there with such abandon ... and there was something so graceful about the curve of her spine and about the way one foot, in its velvet slipper, was touching the floor.... One might almost think that it was a young, blond woman crying.... And her crumpled handkerchief was lying on the carpet just the way it was supposed to, in that pretty scene.

Nikolay uttered a Russian grunt (*kryak*) and sat down on the edge of her couch. He *kryak*'ed again. His mother, still hiding her face, said into the cushion, "Oh, why couldn't you have come earlier? Even one year earlier.... Just one year! ..."

"I wouldn't know," said Nikolay.

"It's all over now," she sobbed, and tossed her light hair. "All over. I'll be fifty in May. Grown-up son comes to see aged mother. And why did you have to come right at this moment ... tonight!"

Nikolay put on his overcoat (which, contrary to European custom, he had simply thrown into a corner), took his cap out of a pocket, and sat down by her again.

"Tomorrow morning I'll move on," he said, stroking the shiny blue silk of his mother's shoulder. "I feel an urge to head north now, to Norway, perhaps—or else out to sea for some whale fishing. I'll write you. In a year or so we'll meet again, then perhaps I'll stay longer. Don't be cross with me because of my wanderlust!"

Quickly she embraced him and pressed a wet cheek to his neck. Then she squeezed his hand and suddenly cried out in astonishment.

"Blown off by a bullet," laughed Nikolay. "Good-bye, my dearest."

She felt the smooth stub of his finger and gave it a cautious kiss. Then she put her arm around her son and walked with him to the door.

[114]

"Please write often.... Why are you laughing? All the powder must have come off my face?"

And no sooner had the door shut after him than she flew, her blue dress rustling, to the telephone.

THE
THUNDERSTORM

Thunder is grom *in Russian, storm is* burya, *and thunderstorm is* groza, *a grand little word, with that blue zigzag in the middle.*

"Groza," written in Berlin, sometime in the summer of 1924, was published in August 1924, in the émigré daily Rul' *and collected in the* Vozvrashchenie Chorba *volume, Slovo, Berlin, 1930.*

At the corner of an otherwise ordinary West Berlin street, under the canopy of a linden in full bloom, I was enveloped by a fierce fragrance. Masses of mist were ascending in the night sky and, when the last star-filled hollow had been absorbed, the wind, a blind phantom, covering his face with his sleeves, swept low through the deserted street. In lusterless darkness, over the iron shutter of a barber shop, its suspended shield—a gilt shaving basin—began swinging like a pendulum.

I came home and found the wind waiting for me in the room: it banged the casement window—and staged a prompt reflux when I shut the door behind me. Under my window there was a deep courtyard where, in the daytime, shirts, crucified on sun-bright clotheslines, shone through the lilac bushes. Out of that yard voices would rise now and then: the melancholy barking of ragmen or empty-bottle buyers; sometimes, the wail of a crippled violin; and, once, an obese blond woman stationed herself in the center of the yard and broke into such lovely song that maids leaned out of all the windows, bending their bare necks. Then, when she had finished, there was a moment of extraordinary still-ness; only my landlady, a slatternly widow, was heard sob-bing and blowing her nose in the corridor.

In that yard now a stifling gloom swelled, but then the

blind wind, which had helplessly slithered into its depths, once again began reaching upward, and suddenly it regained its sight, swept up and, in the amber apertures of the black wall opposite, the silhouettes of arms and disheveled heads began to dart, as escaping windows were being caught and their frames resonantly and firmly locked. The lights went out. The next moment an avalanche of dull sound, the sound of distant thunder, came into motion, and started tumbling through the dark-violet sky. And again all grew still as it had when the beggar woman finished her song, her hands clasped to her ample bosom.

In this silence I fell asleep, exhausted by the happiness of my day, a happiness I cannot describe in writing, and my dream was full of you.

I woke up because the night had begun crashing to pieces. A wild, pale glitter was flying across the sky like a rapid reflection of colossal spokes. One crash after another rent the sky. The rain came down in a spacious and sonorous flow.

I was intoxicated by those bluish tremors, by the keen, volatile chill. I went up to the wet window ledge and inhaled the unearthly air, which made my heart ring like glass.

Ever nearer, ever more grandly, the prophet's chariot rumbled across the clouds. The light of madness, of piercing visions, illumined the nocturnal world, the metal slopes of roofs, the fleeing lilac bushes. The Thunder-god, a white-haired giant with a furious beard, blown back over his shoulder by the wind, dressed in the flying folds of a dazzling raiment, stood, leaning backward, in his fiery chariot, restraining with tensed arms his tremendous, jet-black steeds, their manes a violet blaze. They had broken away from the driver's control, they scattered sparkles of crackling foam, the chariot careened, and the flustered prophet tugged at the reins in vain. His face was distorted by the blast and the strain; the whirlwind, blowing back the folds of his garment, bared a mighty knee; the steeds tossed their blazing manes and rushed on ever more violently, down, down along the clouds. Then, with thunderous hooves, they hurtled across a shiny rooftop, the chariot lurched, Elijah staggered, and the steeds, maddened by the touch of mortal metal, sprang skyward again. The prophet was pitched out. One wheel came off. From my window I saw its enormous fiery hoop roll down the roof, teeter at the edge, and jump off into darkness, while the steeds, dragging the overturned chariot, were already speeding along the highest clouds; the rumble died down, and the stormy blaze vanished in livid chasms.

The Thunder-god, who had fallen onto the roof, rose heavily. His sandals started slipping; he broke a dormer window with his foot, grunted, and, with a sweep of his arm grasped a chimney to steady himself. He slowly turned his frowning face as his eyes searched for something—probably the wheel that had flown off its golden axle. Then he glanced upward, his fingers clutching at his ruffled beard, shook his head crossly—this was probably not the first time that it happened—and, limping slightly, began a cautious descent.

In great excitement I tore myself away from the window, hurried to put on my dressing gown, and ran down the steep staircase straight to the courtyard. The storm had blown over but a waft of rain still lingered in the air. To the east an exquisite pallor was invading the sky.

The courtyard, which from above had seemed to brim with dense darkness, contained, in fact, nothing more than a delicate, melting mist. On its central patch of turf darkened by the damp, a lean, stoop-shouldered old man in a drenched robe stood muttering something and looking around him. Upon seeing me, he blinked angrily and said,

"That you, Elisha?"

I bowed. The prophet clucked his tongue, scratching the while his bald brown spot.

"Lost a wheel. Find it for me, will you?"

The rain had now ceased. Enormous flame-colored clouds collected above the roofs. The shrubs, the fence, the glistening kennel, were floating in the bluish, drowsy air around us. We groped for a long time in various corners. The old man kept grunting, hitching up the heavy hem of his robe, splashing through the puddles with his round-toed sandals, and a bright drop hung from the tip of his large, bony nose. As I brushed aside a low branch of lilac, I noticed, on a pile of rubbish, amid broken glass, a narrow-rimmed iron wheel that must have belonged to a baby carriage. The old man exhaled warm relief above my ear. Hastily, even a little brusquely, he pushed me aside, and snatched up the rusty hoop. With a joyful wink he said, "So that's where it rolled."

Then he stared at me, his white eyebrows came together in a frown, and, as if remembering something, he said in an impressive voice,

"Turn away, Elisha."

I obeyed, even shutting my eyes. I stood like that for a minute or so, and then could not control my curiosity any longer.

The courtyard was empty, except for the old, shaggy dog with its graying muzzle that had thrust its head out of the kennel and was looking up, like a person, with frightened hazel eyes. I looked up too. Elijah had scrambled onto the roof, the iron hoop glimmering behind his back. Above the black chimneys a curly auroral cloud loomed like an orange-hued mountain and, beyond it, a second and a third. The hushed dog and I watched together as the prophet, who had reached the crest of the roof, calmly and unhurriedly stepped upon the cloud and continued to climb, treading heavily on masses of mellow fire. . . .

Sunlight shot through his wheel whereupon it became at once huge and golden, and Elijah himself now seemed robed in flame, blending with the paradisal cloud along which he walked higher and higher until he disappeared in a glorious gorge of the sky.

Only then did the decrepit dog break into a hoarse morning bark. Ripples ran across the bright surface of a rain puddle. The light breeze stirred the geraniums on the balconies. Two or three windows awakened. In my soaked bedslippers and worn dressing gown I ran out into the street to overtake the first, sleepy tramcar, and pulling the skirts of my gown around me, and laughing to myself as I ran, I imagined how, in a few moments, I would be in your house and start telling you about that night's midair accident, and the cross old prophet who fell into my yard.

THE REUNION

Written in Berlin, in December 1931, published in January 1932 under the title Vstrecha (Meeting) *in the émigré daily* Poslednie Novosti, *Paris, and collected in* Soglyadatay, Russkiya Zapiski, *Paris, 1938.*

Lev had a brother, Serafim, who was older and fatter than he, although it was entirely possible that during the past nine years—no, wait, ... God, it was ten, more than ten— he had got thinner, who knows. In a few minutes we shall find out. Lev had left Russia and Serafim had remained, a matter of pure chance in both cases. In fact, you might say that it was Lev who had been leftish, while Serafim, a recent graduate of the Polytechnic Institute, thought of nothing but his chosen field and was wary of political air currents.... How strange, how very strange that in a few minutes he would come in. Was an embrace called for? So many years ... A "*spets*," a specialist. Ah, those words with the chewed-off endings, like discarded fishheads ... "*spets*" ...

There had been a phone call that morning, and an unfamiliar female voice had announced in German that he had arrived, and would like to drop in that evening, as he was leaving again the following day. This had come as a surprise, even though Lev already knew that his brother was in Berlin. Lev had a friend who had a friend, who in turn knew a man who worked at the U.S.S.R. Trade Mission. Serafim had come on an assignment to arrange a purchase of something or other. Was he a Party member? More than ten years ...

All those years they had been out of touch. Serafim knew absolutely nothing about his brother, and Lev knew next to nothing about Serafim. A couple of times Lev caught a glimpse of Serafim's name through the smokescreen grayness of the Soviet papers that he glanced through at the library. "And inasmuch as the fundamental prerequisite of industrialization," spouted Serafim, "is the consolidation of socialist elements in our economic system generally, radical progress in the village emerges as one of the particularly essential and immediate current tasks."

Lev, who had finished his studies with an excusable delay at the University of Prague (his thesis was about Slavophile influences in Russian literature), was now seeking his fortune in Berlin, without ever really being able to decide where that fortune lay: in dealing in various knickknacks, as Leshcheyev advised, or in a printer's job, as Fuchs suggested. Leshcheyev and Fuchs and their wives, by the way, were supposed to come over that evening (it was Russian Christmas). Lev had spent his last bit of cash on a second-hand Christmas tree, fifteen inches tall; a few crimson candles; a pound of zwieback; and half a pound of candy. His guests had promised to take care of the vodka and the wine. However, as soon as he received the conspiratorial, incredible message that his brother wanted to see him, Lev promptly called off the party. The Leshcheyevs were out, and he left word with the maid that something unexpected had come up. Of course, a face-to-face talk with his brother in stark privacy would already be sheer torture, but it would be even worse if ... "This is my brother, he's here from Russia." "Pleased to meet you. Well, are they about ready to croak?" "Whom exactly are you referring to? I don't understand." Leshcheyev was particularly impassioned and intolerant. . . . No, the Christmas party had to be called off.

Now, at about eight in the evening, Lev was pacing his shabby but clean little room, bumping now against the table, now against the white headboard of the lean bed—a needy but neat little man, in a black suit worn shiny and a turn-down collar that was too large for him. His face was beardless, snub-nosed, and not very distinguished, with smallish, slightly mad eyes. He wore spats to hide the holes in his socks. He had recently been separated from his wife, who had quite unexpectedly betrayed him, and with whom! A vulgarian, a nonentity. . . . Now he put away her portrait; otherwise he would have to answer his brother's questions ("Who's that?" "My ex-wife." "What do you mean, ex?"). He removed the Christmas tree too, setting it, with his landlady's permission, out on her balcony—otherwise, who knows, his brother might start making fun of émigré sentimentality. Why had he bought it in the first place? Tradition. Guests, candlelight. Turn off the lamp—let the little tree glow alone. Mirrorlike glints in Mrs. Leshcheyev's pretty eyes.

What would he talk about to his brother? Should he tell him, casually and lightheartedly, about his adventures in the south of Russia at the time of the Civil War? Should he jokingly complain about his present (unbearable, stifling) poverty? Or pretend to be a broadminded man who was above émigré resentment, and understood . . . understood what? That Serafim could have preferred to my poverty, my purity, an active collaboration . . . and with whom, with whom! Or should he, instead, attack him, shame him, argue with him, even be acidly witty? "Grammatically, Leningrad can only mean the town of Nellie."

He pictured Serafim, his meaty, sloping shoulders, his huge rubbers, the puddles in the garden in front of their *dacha*, the death of their parents, the beginning of the Revolution. . . . They had never been particularly close— even when they were at school, each had his own friends, and their teachers were different. . . . In the summer of his seventeenth year Serafim had a rather unsavory affair with a lady from a neighboring *dacha*, a lawyer's wife. The lawyer's hysterical screams, the flying fists, the disarray of the not so young lady, with the catlike face, running down the garden avenue and, somewhere in the background, the disgraceful noise of shattering glass. One day, while swimming in a river, Serafim had nearly drowned. . . . These were Lev's more colorful recollections of his brother, and God knows they didn't amount to much. You often feel that you remember someone vividly and in detail, then you check the matter and it all turns out to be so inane, so meager, so shallow—a deceptive façade, a bogus enterprise on the part of your memory. Nevertheless, Serafim was still his brother. He ate a lot. He was orderly. What else? One evening, at the tea table . . .

The clock struck eight. Lev cast a nervous glance out the window. It was drizzling, and the streetlamps swam in the mist. The white remains of wet snow showed on the sidewalk. Warmed-over Christmas. Pale paper ribbons, left over from the German New Year, hung from a balcony across the street, quivering limply in the dark. The sudden peal of the front-door bell hit Lev like a flash of electricity somewhere in the region of his solar plexus.

He was even bigger and fatter than before. He pretended to be terribly out of breath. He took Lev's hand. Both of them were silent, with identical grins on their faces. A Russian wadded coat, with a small astrakhan collar that fastened with a hook; a gray hat that had been bought abroad.

"Over here," said Lev. "Take it off. Come, I'll put it here. Did you find the house right away?"

"Took the subway," said Serafim, panting. "Well, well. So that's how it is. . . ."

With an exaggerated sigh of relief he sat down in an armchair.

"There'll be some tea ready in a minute," Lev said in a bustling tone as he fussed with a spirit lamp on the sink.

"Foul weather," said Serafim, rubbing his palms together. Actually it was rather warm out.

The alcohol went into a copper sphere; when you turned a thumbscrew it oozed into a black groove. You had to release a tiny amount, turn the screw shut, and light a match. A soft, yellowish flame would appear, floating in the groove, then gradually die, whereupon you opened the valve again, and, with a loud report (—under the iron base where a tall tin teapot bearing a large birthmark on its flank stood with the air of a victim—) a very different, livid flame like a serrated blue crown burst into life. How and why all this happened Lev did not know, nor did the matter interest him. He blindly followed the landlady's instructions. At first Serafim watched the fuss with the spirit lamp over his shoulder, to the extent allowed by his corpulence; then he got up and came closer, and they talked for a while about the apparatus, Serafim explaining its operation and turning the thumbscrew gently back and forth.

"Well, how's life?" he asked, sinking once again into the tight armchair.

"Well—you can see for yourself," replied Lev. "Tea will be ready in a minute. If you're hungry I have some sausage."

Serafim declined, blew his nose thoroughly and started discussing Berlin.

"They've outdone America," he said. "Just look at the traffic. The city has changed enormously. I was here, you know, in '24."

"I was living in Prague at the time," said Lev.

"I see," said Serafim.

Silence. They both watched the teapot, as if they expected some miracle from it.

"It's going to boil soon," said Lev. "Have some of these caramels in the meantime."

Serafim did and his left cheek started working. Lev still could not bring himself to sit down: sitting meant getting set for a chat; he preferred to stand or keep loitering between bed and table, table and sink. Several fir needles lay scattered about the colorless carpet. Suddenly the faint hissing ceased.

"*Prussak kaput*," said Serafim.

"We'll fix that," Lev began in haste, "just one second."

But there was no alcohol left in the bottle. "Stupid situation. . . . You know, I'll go get some from the landlady."

He went out into the corridor and headed for her quarters.—Idiotic. He knocked on the door. No answer. Not an ounce of attention, a pound of contempt. Why did it come to mind, that schoolboy tag (uttered when ignoring a tease)? He knocked again. Everything was dark. She was out. He found his way to the kitchen. The kitchen had been providently locked.

Lev stood for a while in the corridor, thinking not so much about the alcohol as about what a relief it was to be alone for a minute and what agony it would be to return to that tense room where a stranger was securely ensconced. What might one discuss with him? That article on Faraday in an old issue of *Die Natur*? No, that wouldn't do. When he returned Serafim was standing by the bookshelf, examining the tattered, miserable-looking volumes.

"Stupid situation," said Lev. "It's really frustrating. Forgive me, for heaven's sake. Maybe . . ."

(Maybe the water was just about to boil? No. Barely tepid.)

"Nonsense. To be frank, I'm not a great lover of tea. You read a lot, don't you?"

(Should he go downstairs to the pub and get some beer? Not enough money and no credit there. Damn it, he'd blown it all on the candy and the tree.)

"Yes, I do read," he said aloud. "What a shame, what a damn shame. If only the landlady . . ."

"Forget it," said Serafim, "we'll do without. So that's how it is. Yes. And how are things in general? How's your health? Feeling all right? One's health is the main thing. As for me, I don't do much reading," he went on, looking askance at the bookshelf. "Never have enough time. On the train the other day I happened to pick up——"

The phone rang in the corridor.

"Excuse me," said Lev. "Help yourself. Here's the zwieback, and the caramels. I'll be right back." He hurried out.

"What's the matter with you, good sir?" said Leshcheyev's voice. "What's going on here? What happened? Are you sick? What? I can't hear you. Speak up."

"Some unexpected business," replied Lev. "Didn't you get my message?"

"Message my foot. Come on. It's Christmas, the wine's been bought, the wife has a present for you."

"I can't make it," said Lev, "I'm terribly sorry myself. . . ."

"You're a rum fellow! Listen, get out of whatever you're

doing there, and we'll be right over. The Fuchses are here too. Or else, I have an even better idea—you get yourself over here. Eh? Olya, be quiet, I can't hear. What's that?"

"I can't. I have my . . . I'm busy, that's all there is to it."

Leshcheyev emitted a national curse. "Good-bye," said Lev awkwardly into the already dead phone.

Now Serafim's attention had shifted from the books to a picture on the wall.

"Business call. Such a bore," said Lev with a grimace. "Please excuse me."

"You have a lot of business?" asked Serafim, without taking his eyes off the oleograph—a girl in red with a soot-black poodle.

"Well, I make a living—newspaper articles, various stuff," Lev answered vaguely. "And you—so you aren't here for long?"

"I'll probably leave tomorrow. I dropped in to see you for just a few minutes. Tonight I still have to——"

"Sit down, please, sit down. . . ."

Serafim sat down. They remained silent for a while. They were both thirsty.

"We were talking about books," said Serafim. "What with one thing and another I just don't have the time for them. On the train, though, I happened to pick something up, and read it for want of anything better to do. A German novel. Piffle, of course, but rather entertaining. About incest. It went like this. . . ."

He retold the story in detail. Lev kept nodding and looking at Serafim's substantial gray suit, and his ample smooth cheeks, and as he looked he thought: was it really worth having a reunion with your brother after ten years to discuss some philistine tripe by Leonard Frank? It bores him to talk about it and I'm just as bored to listen. Now, let's see, there was something I wanted to say . . . Can't remember. What an agonizing evening.

"Yes, I think I've read it. Yes, that's a fashionable subject these days. Help yourself to some candy. I feel so guilty about the tea. You say you found Berlin greatly changed." (Wrong thing to say—they had already discussed that.)

"The Americanization," answered Serafim. "The traffic. The remarkable buildings."

There was a pause.

"I have something to ask you," said Lev spasmodically. "It's not quite your field, but in this magazine here . . . There were bits I didn't understand. This, for instance—these experiments of his."

Serafim took the magazine and began explaining. "What's so complicated about it? Before a magnetic field is formed —you know what a magnetic field is?—all right, before it is formed, there exists a so-called electric field. Its lines of force are situated in planes that pass through a so-called vibrator. Note that, according to Faraday's teachings, a magnetic line appears as a closed circle, while an electric one is always open. Give me a pencil—no, it's all right, I have one. . . . Thanks, thanks, I have one."

He went on explaining and sketching something for quite a time, while Lev nodded meekly. He spoke of Young, Maxwell, Hertz. A regular lecture. Then he asked for a glass of water.

"It's time for me to be going, you know," he said, licking his lips and setting the glass back on the table. "It's time." From somewhere in the region of his belly he extracted a thick watch. "Yes, it's time."

"Oh, come on, stay a while longer," mumbled Lev, but

Serafim shook his head and got up, tugging down his waist-coat. His gaze stopped once again on the oleograph of the girl in red with the black poodle.

"Do you recall its name?" he asked, with his first genuine smile of the evening.

"Whose name?"

"Oh, you know—Tikhotski used to visit us at the *dacha* with a girl and a poodle. What was the poodle's name?"

"Wait a minute," said Lev. "Wait a minute. Yes, that's right. I'll remember in a moment."

"It was black," said Serafim. "Very much like this one.... Where did you put my coat? Oh, there it is. Got it."

"It's slipped my mind too," said Lev. "Oh, what was the name?"

"Never mind. To hell with it. I'm off. Well ... It was great to see you...." He donned his coat adroitly in spite of his corpulence.

"I'll accompany you," said Lev, producing his frayed raincoat.

Awkwardly, they both cleared their throats at the same instant. Then they descended the stairs in silence and went out. It was drizzling.

"I'm taking the subway. What was that name, though? It was black and had pompons on its paws. My memory is getting incredibly bad."

"There was a 'k' in it," replied Lev. "That much I'm sure of—it had a 'k' in it."

They crossed the street.

"What soggy weather," said Serafim. "Well, well.... So we'll never remember? You say there was a 'k'?"

They turned the corner. Streetlamp. Puddle. Dark post office building. Old beggar woman standing as usual by the stamp machine. She extended a hand with two matchboxes. The beam of the streetlamp touched her sunken cheek; a bright drop quivered under her nostril.

"It's really absurd," exclaimed Serafim. "I know it's there in one of my brain cells, but I can't reach it."

"What was the name . . . what was it?" Lev chimed in. "It really is absurd that we can't . . . Remember how it got lost once, and you and Tikhotski's girl wandered for hours in the woods searching for it. I'm sure there was a 'k' and perhaps an 'r' somewhere."

They reached the square. On its far side shone a pearl horseshoe on blue glass—the emblem of the subway. Stone steps led into the depths.

"She was a stunner, that girl." said Serafim. "Well, I give up. Take care of yourself. Sometime we'll get together again."

"It was something like Turk. . . . Trick . . . No, it won't come. It's hopeless. You also take care of yourself. Good luck."

Serafim gave a wave of his spread hand, and his broad back hunched over and vanished into the depths. Lev started walking back slowly, across the square, past the post office and the beggar woman. . . . Suddenly he stopped short. Somewhere in his memory there was a hint of motion, as if something very small had awakened and begun to stir. The word was still invisible, but its shadow had already crept out as from behind a corner, and he wanted to step on that shadow to keep it from retreating and disappearing again. Alas, he was too late. Everything vanished, but, at the instant his brain ceased straining, the thing stirred again, more perceptibly this time, and like a mouse emerging from a crack when the room is quiet, there appeared, lightly, silently, mysteriously, the live corpuscle of a word. . . . "Give me your paw, Joker." Joker! How simple it was. Joker. . . .

He looked back involuntarily, and thought how Serafim, sitting in his subterranean car, might have remembered too. What a wretched reunion.

Lev heaved a sigh, looked at his watch and, seeing it was not yet too late, decided to head for the Leshcheyevs' house. He would clap his hands under their window, and maybe they would hear and let him in.

A SLICE OF LIFE

The original title of this entertaining tale is Sluchay iz zhizni.
The first word means *"occurrence,"* or *"case,"* and the last two
"from life." The combination has a deliberately commonplace,
newspaper nuance in Russian which is lost in a lexical version. *The*
present formula is truer in English tone especially as it fits so well
my man's primitive jargon (hear his barroom maunder just before
the fracas).

What was your purpose, sir, in penning this story, forty years
ago in Berlin? Well, I did pen it (for I never learned to type and
the long reign of the 3B pencil, capped with an eraser, was to start
much later—in parked motorcars and motels); but I had never any
"purpose" in mind when writing stories—for myself, my wife, and
half a dozen dear dead chuckling friends. It was first published in
Poslednie Novosti, *an émigré daily in Paris, on September 22, 1935,*
and collected three years later in Soglyadatay, Russkiya Zapiski
(*Annales russes, 51, rue de Turbigo, Paris, a legendary address*).

In the next room Pavel Romanovich was roaring with laughter, as he related how his wife had left him.

I could not endure the sound of that horrible hilarity, and without even consulting my mirror, just as I was—in the rumpled dress of a slatternly after-lunch siesta, and no doubt still bearing the pillow's imprint on my cheek—I made for the next room (the dining room of my landlord) and came upon the following scene: my landlord, a person called Plekhanov (totally unrelated to the socialist philosopher) sat listening with an air of encouragement—all the time filling the tubes of Russian cigarettes by means of a tobacco injector—while Pavel Romanovich kept walking around the table, his face a regular nightmare, its pallor seeming to spread to his otherwise wholesome-looking close-shaven head: a very Russian kind of cleanliness, habitually making one think of neat engineer troops, but at the present moment reminding me of something evil, something as frightening as a convict's skull.

He had come, actually, looking for my brother—who had just gone, but this did not really matter to him: his grief had to speak, and so he found a ready listener in this rather unattractive person whom he hardly knew. He laughed, but his eyes did not participate in his guffaws, as he talked of his wife's collecting things all over their flat, of her taking away by some oversight his favorite eyeglasses, of the fact that all her relatives were in the know ahead of him, of his wondering——

"Yes, here's a nice point," he went on, now addressing directly Plekhanov, a God-fearing widower (for his speech until then had been more or less a harangue in sheer space), "a nice, interesting point: how will it be in the hereafter—will she cohabitate there with me or with that swine?"

"Let us go to my room," I said in my most crystalline tone of voice—and only then did he notice my presence: I had stood, leaning forlornly against a corner of the dark sideboard, with which seemed to fuse my diminutive figure in its black dress—yes, I wear mourning, for everybody, for everything, for my own self, for Russia, for the fetuses scraped out of me. He and I passed into the tiny room I rented: it could scarcely accommodate a rather absurdly wide couch covered in silk, and next to it the little low table bearing a lamp whose base was a veritable bomb of thick glass filled with water—and in this atmosphere of my private coziness Pavel Romanovich became at once a different man.

He sat down in silence, rubbing his inflamed eyes. I curled up beside him, patted the cushions around us, and lapsed into thought, cheek-propped feminine thought, as I considered him, his turquoise head, his big strong shoulders which a military tunic would have suited so much better than that doublebreasted jacket. I gazed at him and marveled how I could have been swept off my feet by this short, stocky fellow with insignificant features (except for the teeth—oh my, what fine teeth!); yet I was crazy about him barely two years ago at the beginning of émigré life in Berlin when he was only just planning to marry his goddess—and how very crazy I was, how I wept because of him, how haunted my dreams were by that slender chainlet of steel around his hairy wrist!

He fished out of his hip pocket his massive, "battlefield" (as he termed it) cigarette case. Against its lid, despondently nodding his head, he tapped the tube end of his Russian cigarette several times, more times than he usually did.

"Yes, Maria Vasilevna," he said at last through his teeth as he lit up, raising high his triangular eyebrows. "Yes, nobody could have foreseen such a thing. I had faith in that woman, absolute faith."

After his recent fit of sustained loquacity, everything seemed uncannily quiet. One heard the rain beating against the windowsill, the clicking of Plekhanov's tobacco injector, the whimpering of a neurotic old dog locked up in my brother's room across the corridor. I do not know why—either because the weather was so very gray, or perhaps because the kind of misfortune that had befallen Pavel Romanovich should demand some reaction from the surrounding world (dissolution, eclipse)—but I had the impression that it was late in the evening, though actually it was only three P.M., and I was still supposed to travel to the other end of Berlin on an errand my charming brother could have well done himself.

Pavel Romanovich spoke again, this time in sibilant tones: "That stinking old bitch," he said, "she and she alone pimped them together. I always found her disgusting and didn't conceal it from Lenochka. What a bitch! You've seen her, I think—around sixty, dyed a rich roan, fat, so fat that she looks round-backed. It's a big pity that Nicholas is out. Let him call me as soon as he returns. I am, as you know, a simple, plain-spoken man and I've been telling Lenochka for ages that her mother is an evil bitch. Now here's what I have in mind: perhaps your brother might help me to rig up a letter to the old hag—a sort of formal statement explaining that I know and realize perfectly well whose instigation it was, who nudged my wife—yes, something on those lines, but most politely worded, of course."

I said nothing. Here he was, visiting me for the first time (his visits to Nick did not count), for the first time he sat on my *Kautsch*, and shed cigarette ashes on my polychrome cushions; yet the event, which would formerly have given me divine pleasure, now did not gladden me one bit. Good people had been reporting a long while ago that his marriage had been a flop, that his wife had turned out to be a cheap, skittish fool—and far-sighted rumor had long been giving her a lover in the very person of the freak who had now fallen for her cowish beauty. The news of that wrecked marriage did not, therefore, come to me as a surprise; in fact I may have vaguely expected that some day Pavel Romanovich would be deposited at my feet by a wave of the storm. But no matter how deep I rummaged within myself, I failed to find one crumb of joy; on the contrary, my heart was, oh, so heavy, I simply cannot say how heavy. All my romances, by some kind of collusion between their heroes, have invariably followed a prearranged pattern of mediocrity and tragedy, or more precisely, the tragic slant was imposed by their very mediocrity. I am ashamed to recall the way they started, and appalled by the nastiness of their denouements, while the middle part, the part that should have been the essence and core of this or that affair has remained in my mind as a kind of listless shuffle seen through oozy water or sticky fog. My infatuation with Pavel Romanovich had had at least the delightful advantage of staying cool and lovely in contrast to all the rest; but that infatuation, too, so remote, so deeply buried in the past, was borrowing now from the present, in reverse order, a tinge of misfortune, failure, even plain mortification, just because I was forced to hear this man's complaining of his wife, of his mother-in-law.

"I do hope," he said, "Nicky comes back soon. I have still another plan in reserve, and, I think, it's quite a good one. And in the meantime I'd better toddle along."

And still I said nothing, in great sadness looking at him, my lips masked by the fringe of my black shawl. He stood for a moment by the windowpane, on which in tumbling motion, knocking and buzzing, a fly went up, up, and presently slid down again. Then he passed his finger across the spines of the books on my shelf. Like most people who read little, he had a sneaking affection for dictionaries, and now he pulled out a thick-bottomed pink volume with the seed head of a dandelion and a red-curled girl on the cover.

"*Khoroshaya shtooka*" he said—crammed back the *shtooka* (thing), and suddenly broke into tears. I had him sit down close to me on the couch, he swayed to one side with his sobs increasing, and ended by burying his face in my lap. I stroked lightly his hot emery-papery scalp and rosy robust nape which I find so attractive in males. Gradually his spasms abated. He bit me softly through my skirt, and sat up.

"Know what?" said Pavel Romanovich and while speaking he sonorously clacked together the concave palms of his horizontally placed hands (I could not help smiling as I remembered an uncle of mine, a Volga landowner, who used to render that way the sound of a procession of dignified cows letting their pies plop). "Know what, my dear?

Let us move to my flat. I can't stand the thought of being there alone. We'll have supper there, take a few swigs of vodka, then go to the movies—what do you say?"

I could not decline his offer, though I knew that I would regret it. While telephoning to cancel my visit to Nick's former place of employment (he needed the rubber overshoes he had left there), I saw myself in the looking-glass of the hallway as resembling a forlorn little nun with a stern waxy face; but a minute later, as I was in the act of prettying up and putting on my hat, I plunged as it were into the depth of my great, black, experienced eyes, and found therein a gleam of something far from nunnish—even through my voilette they blazed, good God, how they blazed!

In the tram, on the way to his place, Pavel Romanovich became distant and gloomy again: I was telling him about Nick's new job in the ecclesiastical library, but his gaze kept shifting, he was obviously not listening. We arrived. The disorder in the three smallish rooms which he had occupied with his Lenochka was simply incredible—as if his and her things had had a thorough fight. In order to amuse Pavel Romanovich I started to play the soubrette, I put on a diminutive apron that had been forgotten in a corner of the kitchen, I introduced peace in the disarray of the furniture, I laid the table most neatly—so that Pavel Romanovich slapped his hands together once more and decided to make some borshch (he was quite proud of his cooking abilities).

After two or three ponies of vodka, his mood became inordinately energetic and pseudo-efficient, as if there really existed a certain project that had to be attended to now. I am at a loss to decide whether he had got self-infected by the theatrical solemnity with which a stalwart expert in drinking is able to decorate the intake of Russian liquor, or whether he really believed that he and I had begun, when still in my room, to plan and discuss something or other—but there he was, filling his fountain pen and with a significant air bringing out what he called the dossier: letters from his wife received by him last spring in Bremen where he had gone on behalf of the émigré insurance company for which he worked. From these letters he began to cite passages proving she loved *him* and not the other chap. In between he kept repeating brisk little formulas such as "That's that," "Okey-dokey," "Let's see now"—and went on drinking. His argument reduced itself to the idea that if Lenochka wrote: 'I caress you mentally, Baboonovich dear' she could not be in love with another man, and if she thought she was, her error should be patiently explained to her. After a few more drinks his manner changed, his expression grew somber and coarse. For no reason at all, he took off his shoes and his socks, and then started to sob and walked sobbing, from one end of his flat to the other, absolutely ignoring my presence and ferociously kicking aside with a strong bare foot the chair into which he kept barging. En passant, he managed to finish the decanter, and presently entered a third phase, the final part of that drunken syllogism which had already united, in keeping with strict dialectical rules, an initial show of bright efficiency and a central period of utter gloom. At the present stage, it appeared that he and I had established something (what exactly, remained rather blurry) that displayed her lover as the lowest of villains, and the plan consisted in my going to see her on my own initiative, as it were, to "warn" her. It was also to be understood that Pavel Romanovich remained absolutely opposed to any intrusion or pressure and that his own suggestions bore the stamp of angelic disinterestedness. Before I could disentangle my wits, already tightly enveloped in the web of his thick whisper (while he was hastily putting on his shoes), I found myself getting his wife on the phone and only when I heard her high, stupidly resonant voice did I suddenly realize that I was drunk and behaving like an idiot. I slammed down the receiver, but he started to kiss my cold hands which I kept clenching—and I called her again, was identified without enthusiasm, said I had to see her on a piece of urgent business, and after some slight hesitation she agreed to have me come over at once. By that time—that is by the time he and I had started to go, our plan, it transpired, had ripened in every detail and was amazingly simple. I was to tell Lenochka that Pavel Romanovich had to convey to her something of exceptional importance—in no way, in no way whatever, related to their broken marriage (this he forcibly stressed, with a tactician's special appetite) and that he would be awaiting her in the bar just across her street.

It took me ages, dim ages, to climb the staircase, and for some reason I was terribly tormented by the thought that at our last meeting I wore the same hat and the same black fox. Lenochka, on the other hand, came out to me smartly dressed. Her hair seemed to have just been curled, but curled badly, and in general she had grown plainer, and about her chicly painted mouth there were puffy little pouches owing to which all that chic was rather lost.

"I do not believe one minute," she said, surveying me with curiosity, "that it is all that important, but if he thinks we haven't done arguing, fine, I agree to come, but I want it to be before witnesses, I'm scared to remain alone with him, I've had enough of that, thank you very much."

When we entered the pub, Pavel Romanovich sat leaning on his elbow at a table next to the bar; he rubbed with his minimus his red naked eyes, while imparting at length, in monotone, some "slice of life," as he liked to put it, to a total stranger seated at the same table, a German, enormously tall, with sleekly parted hair but a black-downed nape and badly bitten fingernails.

"However," Pavel Romanovich was saying in Russian, "my father did not wish to get into trouble with the authorities and therefore decided to build a fence around it. Okay, that was settled. Our house was about as far from theirs as—" He looked around, nodded absentmindedly to his wife, and continued in a perfectly relaxed manner—"As far as from here to the tramway, so that they could not have any claims. But you must agree, that spending the entire autumn in Vilna without electricity is no joking matter. Well, then, most reluctantly——"

I found it impossible to understand what he was talking about. The German listened dutifully, with half-opened mouth: his knowledge of Russian was scanty, the sheer process of trying to understand afforded him pleasure. Lenochka, who was sitting so close to me that I sensed her disagreeable warmth, began to rummage in her bag.

"My father's illness," went on Pavel Romanovich, "contributed to his decision. If you really lived there, as you say, then you remember, of course, that street. It is dark there by night, and not infrequently one happens to read——"

"Pavlik," said Lenochka, "here's your pince-nez, I took it away in my bag by mistake."

"It is dark there by night," repeated Pavel Romanovich, opening as he spoke the spectacle case that she had tossed to him across the table. He put on the eyeglasses, produced a revolver and started to shoot at his wife.

With a great howl she fell under the table dragging me

after her while the German stumbled over us and joined us in our fall so that the three of us sort of got mixed up on the floor; but I had time to see a waiter rush up to the aggressor from behind and with monstrous relish and force hit him on the head with an iron ashtray. After this there was as usual in such cases the slow tidying up of the shattered world, with the participation of gapers, policemen, ambulancers. Extravagantly groaning, Lenochka (a bullet had merely gone through her fat sun-tanned shoulder) was driven away to the hospital, but somehow I did not see how they led Pavel Romanovich away. By the time everything was over—that is by the time everything had reoccupied its right place: streetlamps, houses, stars, I found myself walking on a deserted sidewalk in the company of our German survivor: that huge handsome man, hatless, in a voluminous raincoat floated beside me and at first I thought he was seeing me home but then it dawned upon me that we were heading for *his* place. We stopped in front of his house, and he explained to me—slowly, weightily but not without a certain shade of poetry, and for some reason in bad French—that he could not take me to his room because he lived with a chum who replaced for him a father, a brother, and a wife. His excuses struck me as so insulting that I ordered him to call a taxi at once and take me to my lodgings. He smiled a frightened smile and closed the door in my face, and there I was walking along a street which despite the rain's having stopped hours ago, was still wet and conveyed an air of deep humiliation—yes, there I was walking all alone as was my due to walk from the beginning of time, and before my eyes Pavel Romanovich kept rising, rising and rubbing off the blood and the ash from his poor head.

CHRISTMAS

Rozhdestvo *was written in Berlin, at the end of 1924, published in the* Rul' *in two installments, January 6 and 8, 1925, and collected in* Vozvrashchenie Chorba, Slovo, *Berlin, 1930. It oddly resembles the type of chess problem called "selfmate."*

1

After walking back from the village to his manor across the dimming snows, Sleptsov sat down in a corner, on a plush-covered chair which he never remembered using before. It was the kind of thing that happens after some great calamity. Not your brother but a chance acquaintance, a vague country neighbor to whom you never paid much attention, with whom in normal times you exchange scarcely a word, is the one who comforts you wisely and gently, and hands you your dropped hat after the funeral service is over, and you are reeling from grief, your teeth chattering, your eyes blinded by tears. The same can be said of inanimate objects. Any room, even the coziest and the most absurdly small, in the little used wing of a great country house has an unlived-in corner. And it was such a corner in which Sleptsov sat.

The wing was connected by a wooden gallery, now encumbered with our huge north Russian snowdrifts, to the master house, used only in summer. There was no need to awaken it, to heat it: the master had come from Petersburg for only a couple of days and had settled in the annex, where it was a simple matter to get the stoves of white Dutch tile going.

The master sat in his corner, on that plush chair, as in a doctor's waiting room. The room floated in darkness; the dense blue of early evening filtered through the crystal feathers of frost on the windowpane. Ivan, the quiet, portly valet, who had recently shaved off his mustache and now looked like his late father, the family butler, brought in a kerosene lamp, all trimmed and brimming with light. He set it on a small table, and noiselessly caged it within its pink silk shade. For an instant a tilted mirror reflected his lit ear and cropped gray hair. Then he withdrew and the door gave a subdued creak.

Sleptsov raised his hand from his knee and slowly examined it. A drop of candle wax had stuck and hardened in the thin fold of skin between two fingers. He spread his fingers and the little white scale cracked.

2

The following morning, after a night spent in nonsensical, fragmentary dreams totally unrelated to his grief, as Sleptsov stepped out into the cold veranda, a floorboard emitted a merry pistol crack underfoot, and the reflections of the many-colored panes formed paradisal lozenges on the white-washed cushionless window seats. The outer door resisted at first, then opened with a luscious crunch, and the dazzling frost hit his face. The reddish sand providently sprinkled on the ice coating the porch steps resembled cinnamon, and thick icicles shot with greenish blue hung from the eaves. The snowdrifts reached all the way to the windows of the annex, tightly gripping the snug little wooden structure in their frosty clutches. The creamy white mounds of what were flower beds in summer swelled slightly above the level snow in front of the porch, and further off loomed the radiance of the park, where every black branchlet was rimmed with silver, and the firs seemed to draw in their green paws under their bright plump load.

[154]

Wearing high felt boots and a short fur-lined coat with a karakul collar, Sleptsov strode off slowly along a straight path, the only one cleared of snow, into that blinding distant landscape. He was amazed to be still alive, and able to perceive the brilliance of the snow and feel his front teeth ache from the cold. He even noticed that a snow-covered bush resembled a fountain and that a dog had left a series of saffron marks on the slope of a snowdrift, which had burned through its crust. A little further, the supports of a foot bridge stuck out of the snow, and there Sleptsov stopped. Bitterly, angrily, he pushed the thick, fluffy covering off the parapet. He vividly recalled how this bridge looked in summer. There was his son walking along the slippery planks, flecked with aments, and deftly plucking off with his net a butterfly that had settled on the railing. Now the boy sees his father. Forever lost laughter plays on his face, under the turned-down brim of a straw hat burned dark by the sun; his hand toys with the chainlet of the leather purse attached to his belt, his dear, smooth, suntanned legs in their serge shorts and soaked sandals assume their usual cheerful wide-spread stance. Just recently, in Petersburg, after having babbled in his delirium about school, about his bicycle, about some great Oriental moth, he died, and yesterday Sleptsov had taken the coffin— weighed down, it seemed, with an entire lifetime—to the country, into the family vault near the village church.

It was quiet as it can only be on a bright, frosty day. Sleptsov raised his leg high, stepped off the path and, leaving blue pits behind him in the snow, made his way among the trunks of amazingly white trees to the spot where the park dropped off toward the river. Far below, ice blocks sparkled near a hole cut in the smooth expanse of white and, on the opposite bank, very straight columns of pink smoke stood above the snowy roofs of log cabins. Sleptsov took off his karakul cap and leaned against a tree trunk. Somewhere far away peasants were chopping wood —every blow bounced resonantly skyward—and beyond the light silver mist of trees, high above the squat izbas, the sun caught the equanimous radiance of the cross on the church.

3

That was where he headed after lunch, in an old sleigh with a high straight back. The cod of the black stallion clacked strongly in the frosty air, the white plumes of low branches glided overhead, and the ruts in front gave off a silvery blue sheen. When he arrived he sat for an hour or so by the grave, resting a heavy, woolen-gloved hand on the iron of the railing that burned his hand through the wool. He came home with a slight sense of disappointment, as if there, in the burial vault, he had been even further removed from his son than here, where the countless summer tracks of his rapid sandals were preserved beneath the snow.

In the evening, overcome by a fit of intense sadness, he had the main house unlocked. When the door swung open with a weighty wail, and a whiff of special, unwintery coolness came from the sonorous iron-barred vestibule, Sleptsov took the lamp with its tin reflector from the watchman's hand and entered the house alone. The parquet floors crackled eerily under his step. Room after room filled with yellow light, and the shrouded furniture seemed unfamiliar; instead of a tinkling chandelier, a soundless bag hung from the ceiling; and Sleptsov's enormous shadow, slowly extending one arm, floated across the wall and over the gray squares of curtained paintings.

He went into the room which had been his son's study in summer, set the lamp on the window ledge and, breaking his fingernails as he did so, opened the folding shutters, even though all was darkness outside. In the blue glass the yellow flame of the slightly smoky lamp appeared, and his large, bearded face showed momentarily.

He sat down at the bare desk and sternly, from under bent brows, examined the pale wallpaper with its garlands of bluish roses; a narrow officelike cabinet, with sliding drawers from top to bottom; the couch and armchairs under slipcovers; and suddenly, dropping his head onto the desk, he started to shake, passionately, noisily, pressing first his lips, then his wet cheek, to the cold, dusty wood and clutching at its far corners.

In the desk he found a notebook, spreading boards, supplies of black pins and an English biscuit tin that contained a large exotic cocoon which had cost three rubles. It was papery to the touch and seemed made of a brown folded leaf. His son had remembered it during his sickness, regretting that he had left it behind, but consoling himself with the thought that the chrysalid inside was probably dead. He also found a torn net: a tarlatan bag on a collapsible hoop (and the muslin still smelled of summer and sun-hot grass).

Then, bending lower and lower and sobbing with his whole body, he began pulling out one by one the glass-topped drawers of the cabinet. In the dim lamplight the even files of specimens shone silklike under the glass. Here, in this room, on that very desk, his son had spread the wings of his captures. He would first pin the carefully killed insect in the cork-bottomed groove of the setting board, between the adjustable strips of wood, and fasten down flat with pinned strips of paper the still fresh, soft wings. They had now dried long ago and been transferred to the cabinet—those spectacular Swallowtails, those dazzling Coppers and Blues, and the various Fritillaries, some mounted in a supine position to display the mother-of-pearl undersides. His son used to pronounce their Latin names with a moan of triumph or in an arch aside of disdain. And the moths, the moths, the first Aspen Hawk of five summers ago!

4

The night was smoke-blue and moonlit; thin clouds were scattered about the sky but did not touch the delicate, icy moon. The trees, masses of gray frost, cast dark shadows on the drifts, which scintillated here and there with metallic sparks. In the plush-upholstered, well-heated room of the annex Ivan had placed a two-foot fir tree in a clay pot on the table, and was just attaching a candle to its cruciform tip when Sleptsov returned from the main house, chilled, red-eyed, with gray dust smears on his cheek, carrying a wooden case under his arm. Seeing the Christmas tree on the table, he asked absently:

"What's that?"

Relieving him of the case, Ivan answered in a low, mellow voice:

"There's a holiday coming up tomorrow."

"No, take it away," said Sleptsov with a frown, while thinking, "Can this be Christmas Eve? How could I have forgotten?"

Ivan gently insisted:

"It's nice and green. Let it stand for a while."

"Please take it away," repeated Sleptsov, and bent over the case he had brought. In it he had gathered his son's belongings—the folding butterfly net, the biscuit tin with the pear-shaped cocoon, the spreading board, the pins in their lacquered box, the blue notebook. Half of the first page had been torn out, and its remaining fragment contained part of a French dictation. There followed daily entries, names of captured butterflies, and other notes:

"Walked across the bog as far as Borovichi, . . ."

"Raining today. Played checkers with Father, then read Goncharov's *Frigate*, a deadly bore."

"Marvelous hot day. Rode my bike in the evening. A midge got in my eye. Deliberately rode by her dacha twice, but didn't see her. . . ."

Sleptsov raised his head, swallowed something hot and huge. Of whom was his son writing?

"Rode my bike as usual," he read on, "Our eyes nearly met. My darling, my love. . . ."

"This is unthinkable," whispered Sleptsov. "I'll never know. . . ."

He bent over again, avidly deciphering the childish handwriting that slanted up then curved down in the margin.

"Saw a fresh specimen of the Camberwell Beauty today. That means autumn is here. Rain in the evening. She has probably left, and we didn't even get acquainted. Farewell, my darling. I feel terribly sad. . . ."

"He never said anything to me...." Sleptsov tried to remember, rubbing his forehead with his palm.

On the last page there was an ink drawing: the hind view of an elephant—two thick pillars, the corners of two ears, and a tiny tail.

Sleptsov got up. He shook his head, restraining yet another onrush of hideous sobs.

"I–can't–bear–it–any–longer," he drawled between groans, repeating even more slowly, "I—can't—bear—it—any—longer...."

"It's Christmas tomorrow," came the abrupt reminder, "and I'm going to die. Of course. It's so simple. This very night...."

He pulled out a handkerchief and dried his eyes, his beard, his cheeks. Dark streaks remained on the handkerchief.

"... death," Sleptsov said softly, as if concluding a long sentence.

The clock ticked. Frost patterns overlapped on the blue glass of the window. The open notebook shone radiantly on the table; next to it the light went through the muslin of the butterfly net, and glistened on a corner of the open tin. Sleptsov pressed his eyes shut, and had a fleeting sensation that earthly life lay before him, totally bared and comprehensible—and ghastly in its sadness, humiliatingly pointless, sterile, devoid of miracles....

At that instant there was a sudden snap—a thin sound like that of an overstretched rubber band breaking. Sleptsov opened his eyes. The cocoon in the biscuit tin had burst at its tip, and a black, wrinkled creature the size of a mouse was crawling up the wall above the table. It stopped, holding on to the surface with six black furry feet, and started palpitating strangely. It had emerged from the chrysalid because a man overcome with grief had transferred a tin box to his warm room, and the warmth had penetrated its taut leaf-and-silk envelope; it had awaited this moment so long, had collected its strength so tensely, and now, having broken out, it was slowly and miraculously expanding. Gradually the wrinkled tissues, the velvety fringes, unfurled; the fan-pleated veins grew firmer as they filled with air. It became a winged thing imperceptibly, as a maturing face imperceptibly becomes beautiful. And its wings—still feeble, still moist—kept growing and unfolding, and now they were developed to the limit set for them by God, and there, on the wall, instead of a little lump of life, instead of a dark mouse, was a great *Attacus* moth like those that fly, birdlike, around lamps in the Indian dusk.

And then those thick black wings, with a glazy eyespot on each and a purplish bloom dusting their hooked foretips, took a full breath under the impulse of tender, ravishing, almost human happiness.

A BUSY MAN

The Russian original (Zanyatoy chelovek), *written in Berlin between the 17th and the 26th of September, 1931, appeared on October the 20th in the émigré daily* Poslednie Novosti, Paris, *and was included in the collection* Soglyadatay, Russkiya Zapiski, Paris, *1938.*

The man who busies himself overmuch with the workings of his own soul cannot help being confronted by a common, melancholy, but rather curious phenomenon: namely, he witnesses the sudden death of an insignificant memory that a chance occasion causes to be brought back from the humble and remote almshouse where it had been completing quietly its obscure existence. It blinks, it is still pulsating and reflecting light—but the next moment, under your very eyes, it breathes one last time and turns up its poor toes, having not withstood the too abrupt transit into the harsh glare of the present. Henceforth all that remains at your disposal is the shadow, the abridgment of that recollection, now devoid, alas, of the original's bewitching convincingness. Grafitski, a gentle-tempered and death-fearing person, remembered a boyhood dream which had contained a laconic prophecy; but he had ceased long ago to feel any organic link between himself and that memory, for at one of the first summonses, it arrived looking wan, and died—and the dream he now remembered was but the recollection of a recollection. When was it, that dream? Exact date unknown. Grafitski answered, pushing away the little glass pot with smears of yogurt and leaning his elbow on the table. When? Come on—approximately? A long time ago. Presumably, between the ages of ten and fifteen:

during that period he often thought about death—especially at night.

So here he is—a thirty-two-year-old, smallish, but broad-shouldered man, with protruding transparent ears, half-actor, half-literatus, author of topical jingles in the émigré papers over a not very witty pen name (unpleasantly reminding one of the "Caran d'Ache" adopted by an immortal cartoonist). Here he is. His face consists of horn-framed dark glasses, with a blindman's glint in them, and of a soft-tufted wart on the left cheek. His head is balding and through the straight strands of brushed-back dunnish hair one discerns the pale-pink shammy of his scalp.

What had he been thinking about just now? What was the recollection under which his jailed mind kept digging? The recollection of a dream. The warning addressed to him in a dream. A prediction, which up to now had in no way hampered his life, but which at present, at the inexorable approach of a certain deadline, was beginning to sound with an insistent, ever-increasing resonance.

"You must control yourself," cried Itski to Graf in a hysterical recitative. He cleared his throat and walked to the closed window.

An ever-increasing insistence. The figure 33—the theme of that dream—had got entangled with his unconscious, its curved claws like those of a bat, had got caught in his soul, and there was no way to unravel that subliminal snarl. According to tradition, Jesus Christ lived to the age of thirty-three and perhaps (mused Graf, immobilized next to the cross of the casement frame), perhaps a voice in that dream had indeed said: 'You'll die at Christ's age'—and had displayed, illumined upon a screen, the thorns of two tremendous threes.

He opened the window. It was lighter without than

within, but streetlamps had already started to glow. Smooth clouds blanketed the sky; and only westerwards, between ochery housetops, an interspace was banded with tender brightness. Farther up the street a fiery-eyed automobile had stopped, its straight tangerine tusks plunged in the watery gray of the asphalt. A blond butcher stood on the threshold of his shop and contemplated the sky.

As if crossing a stream from stone to stone, Graf's mind jumped from butcher to carcass and then to somebody who had been telling him that somebody else somewhere (in a morgue? At a medical school?) used to call a corpse fondly: the "smully" or "smullicans." He's waiting around the corner, your "smullicans." Don't you worry: "smully" won't let you down.

"Allow me to sort out various possibilities," said Graf with a snigger as he looked down askance from his fifth floor at the black iron spikes of a palisade. "Number one (the most vexing): I dream of the house being attacked or on fire, I leap out of bed and, thinking (we are fools in sleep) that I live at street level, I dive out of the window—into an abyss. Second possibility: in a different nightmare I swallow my tongue—that's known to have happened—the fat thing performs a back somersault in my mouth and I suffocate. Case number three: I'm roaming, say, through noisy streets—aha, that's Pushkin trying to imagine his way of death:

> In combat, wanderings or waves,
> Or will it be the nearby valley . . .

etc., but mark—he began with 'combat,' which means he did have a presentiment. Superstition may be masked wisdom. What can I do to stop thinking those thoughts? What can I do in my loneliness?"

He married in 1924, in Riga, coming from Pskov with a skimpy theatrical company. Was the coupleteer of the show—and when before his act he took off his spectacles to touch up with paint his deadish little face one saw that he had eyes of a smoky blue. His wife was a large, robust woman with short black hair, a glowing complexion and a fat prickly nape. Her father sold furniture. Soon after marrying her Graf discovered that she was stupid and coarse, that she had bow legs, and that for every two Russian words she used a dozen German ones. He realized that they must separate, but deferred the decision because of a kind of dreamy compassion he felt for her and so things dragged until 1926 when she deceived him with the owner of a delicatessen on Lachplesis street. Graf moved from Riga to Berlin where he was promised a job in a film-making firm (which soon folded up). He led an indigent, disorganized, solitary life and spent hours in a cheap pub where he wrote his topical poems. This was the pattern of his life—a life that made little sense—the meager, vapid existence of a third-rate Russian émigré. But as is well known, consciousness is not determined by this or that way of life. In times of comparative ease as well as on such days when one goes hungry and one's clothes begin to rot, Grafitski lived not unhappily—at least before the approach of the fateful year. With perfect good sense he could be called a "busy man," for the subject of his occupation was his own soul—and in such cases, there can be no question of leisure or indeed any necessity for it. We are discussing the air holes of life, a dropped heartbeat, pity, the irruptions of past things—what fragrance is that? What does it remind me of? And why does no one notice that on the dullest street every house is different, and what a profusion there is, on buildings, on furniture, on every object, of seemingly useless ornaments—yes, useless, but full of disinterested, sacrificial enchantment.

Let us speak frankly. There is many a person whose soul has gone to sleep like a leg. Per contra, there exist people endowed with principles, ideals—sick souls gravely affected by problems of faith and morality; they are not artists of sensibility, but the soul is their mine where they dig and drill, working deeper and deeper with the coal-cutting machine of religious conscience and getting giddy from the black dust of sins, small sins, pseudo-sins. Graf did not belong to their group: he lacked any special sins and had no special principles. He busied himself with his individual self, as others study a certain painter, or collect certain mites or decipher manuscripts rich in complex transpositions and insertions, with doodles, like hallucinations, in the margin, and temperamental deletions that burn the bridges between masses of imagery—bridges whose restoration is such wonderful fun.

His studies were now interrupted by alien considerations —this was unexpected and dreadfully painful—what should be done about it? After lingering by the window (and doing his best to find some defense against the ridiculous, trivial, but invincible idea that in a few days, on June the 19th, he would have attained the age mentioned in his boyhood dream), Graf quietly left his darkening room, in which all objects, buoyed up slightly by the waves of the crepuscule, no longer stood, but floated, like furniture during a great flood. It was still day—and somehow one's heart contracted from the tenderness of early lights. Graf noticed at once that not all was right, that a strange agitation was spreading around: people gathered at the corners of streets, made mysterious angular signals, walked over to the opposite side, and there again pointed at something afar and then stood motionless in eerie attitudes of torpor. In the twilight dimness, nouns were lost, only verbs remained—or at least the archaic forms of a few verbs. This kind of thing might mean a lot: for example, the end of the world. Suddenly with a numbing tingle in every part of his frame, he understood: There, there, across the deep vista between buildings, outlined softly against a clear golden background, under the lower rim of a long ashen cloud, very low, very far, and very slowly, and also ash-colored, also elongated, an airship was floating by. The exquisite, antique loveliness of its motion, mating with the intolerable beauty of the evening sky, tangerine lights, blue silhouettes of people, caused the contents of Graf's soul to brim over. He saw it as a celestial token, an old-fashioned apparition, reminding him that he was on the point of reaching the established limit of his life; he read in his mind the inexorable obituary: our valuable collaborator ... so early in life ... we who knew him so well ... fresh humor ... fresh grave. ... And what was still more inconceivable: all around that obituary, to paraphrase Pushkin again, ... *indifferent nature would be shining*—the flora of a newspaper, weeds of domestic news, burdocks of editorials.

On a quiet summer night he turned thirty-three. Alone in his room, clad in long underpants, striped like those of a convict, glassless and blinking, he celebrated his unbidden birthday. He had not invited anybody because he feared such contingencies as a broken pocket mirror or some talk about life's fragility, which the retentive mind of a guest would be sure to promote to the rank of an omen. Stay, stay, moment—thou art not as fair as Goethe's—but nevertheless stay. Here we have an unrepeatable individual in an unrepeatable medium: the storm-felled worn books on the shelves, the little glass pot of yogurt (said to lengthen life), the tufted brush for cleaning one's pipe, the stout album of an ashen tint in which Graf pasted everything, beginning with the clippings of his verse and finishing with a Russian tram ticket—these are the surroundings of Graf Ytski (a pen-name he had thought up on a rainy night while waiting for the next ferry), a butterfly-eared, husky little man who sat on the edge of his bed holding the holey violet sock he had just taken off.

Henceforth he began to fear everything—the lift, a draught, builder's scaffolds, the traffic, demonstrators, a truck-mounted platform for the repairing of trolley wires, the colossal dome of the gashouse that might explode right when he passed by on his way to the post office, where, furthermore, a bold bandit in a homemade mask might go on a shooting spree. He realized the silliness of his state of mind but was unable to overcome it. In vain did he try to divert his attention, to think of something else: on the footboard at the back of every thought that went speeding by like a sledded carriage stood Smully, the ever-present groom. On the other hand the topical poems with which he continued diligently to supply the papers became more and more playful and artless (since nobody should note in them retrospectively the presentiment of nearing death), and those wooden couplets whose rhythm recalled the see-saw of the Russian toy featuring a muzhik and a bear, and in which "shrilly" rhymed with "Dzhugashvili"—those couplets, and not anything else, turned out to be actually the most substantial and fitly piece of his being.

Naturally, faith in the immortality of the soul is not forbidden; but there is one terrible question which nobody to my knowledge has set (mused Graf over a mug of beer): may not the soul's passage into the hereafter be attended with the possibility of random impediments and vicissitudes similar to the various mishaps surrounding a person's birth in this world? Cannot one help that passage to succeed by taking while still alive certain psychological or even physical measures? Which specifically? What must one foresee, what must one stock, what must one avoid? Should one regard religion (argued Graf, dallying in the deserted darkened pub where the chairs were already yawning and being put to bed on the tables)—religion, which covers the walls of life with sacred pictures—as something on the lines of that attempt to create a favorable setting (rather in the same way as, according to certain physicians, the photographs of professional babies, with nice, chubby cheeks, by adorning the bedroom of a pregnant woman act beneficially on the fruit of her womb)? But even if the necessary measures have been taken, even if we do know why Mr. X (who fed on this or that—milk, music—or whatever) safely crossed over into the hereafter, while Mr. Y. (whose nourishment was slightly different) got stuck and perished —might there not exist other hazards capable of occurring at the very moment of passing over—and somehow getting in one's way, spoiling everything—for, mind you, even animals or plain people creep away when their hour approaches: do not hinder, do not hinder me in my difficult, perilous task, allow me to be delivered peacefully of my immortal soul.

All this depressed Graf, but meaner yet and more terrible was the thought of there not being any "hereafter" at all, that a man's life bursts as irremediably as the bubbles that dance and vanish in a tempestuous tub under the jaws of a rainpipe—Graf watched them from the veranda of a suburban café—it was raining hard, autumn had come, four months had elapsed since he had reached the fatidic age, death might hit any minute now—and those trips to the dismal pine barrens near Berlin were extremely risky. "If, however," thought Graf, "there is no hereafter, then away with it goes everything else that involves the idea of an independent soul, away goes the possibility of omens and presentiments; all right, let us be materialists, and therefore, I, a healthy individual with a healthy heredity shall, probably, live half a century more, and so why yield to neurotic illusions—they are only the result of a certain temporary instability of my social class, and the individual is immortal inasmuch as his class is immortal—and the great class of the bourgeoisie (continued Graf, now thinking aloud with disgusting animation), our great and powerful class shall conquer the hydra of the proletariat, for we, too, slave-owners, corn merchants, and their loyal troubadours, must step onto the platform of our class (more zip, please), we all, the bourgeois of all countries, the bourgeois of all lands . . . and nations, arise, our oil-mad (or gold-mad?) *kollektiv*, down with plebeian miscreations—and now any verbal adverb ending in '*iv*' will do as a rhyme; after that two more strophes and again: up, bourgeois of all lands and nations! long live our sacred *kapitál*! Tra-ta-ta (anything in '-ations'), our bourgeois *Internatsionál*! Is the result witty? Is it amusing?"

Winter came. Graf borrowed fifty marks from a neighbor and used the money to eat his fill, since he was not prepared to allow fate the slightest loophole. That odd neighbor, who of his own (his own!) accord had offered financial assistance, was a newcomer occupying the two best rooms of the fifth floor, called Ivan Ivanovich Engel—a sort of stoutish gentleman with gray locks, resembling the accepted type of a composer or chess maestro, but in point of fact, representing some kind of foreign (very foreign, perhaps, Far-Eastern or Celestial) firm. When they happened to meet in the corridor he smiled kindly, shyly, and poor Graf explained this sympathy by assuming his neighbor to be a businessman of no culture, remote from literature and other mountain resorts of the human spirit, and thus instinctively bearing for him, Grafitski the Dreamer, a delicious thrilling esteem. Anyway, Graf had too many troubles to pay much attention to his neighbor, but in a rather absentminded way he kept availing himself of the old gentleman's angelic nature—and on nights of unendurable nicotinelessness, for example, would knock at Mr. Engel's door and obtain a cigar—but did not really grow chummy with him and, indeed, never asked him in (except that time when the desk lamp burned out, and the landlady had chosen that evening for going to the cinema, and the neighbor brought a brand new bulb and delicately screwed it in).

On Christmas Graf was invited by some literary friends to a *yolka* (fir tree) and through the motley talk told himself with a sinking heart that he saw those colored baubles for the last time. Once, in the middle of a serene February night, he kept looking too long at the firmament and suddenly felt unable to suffer the burden and pressure of human consciousness, that ominous and ludicrous luxury: a detestable spasm made him gasp for breath, and the monstrous star-stained sky swung into motion. Graf curtained the window and, holding one hand to his heart, knocked with the other at Ivan Engel's door. The latter, with a mild smile and a slight German accent, offered him some *valerianka*. It so happened, by the way, that when Graf entered, he caught Mr. Engel standing in the middle of his bedroom and distilling the calmative into a wineglass—no doubt for his own use: holding the glass in his right hand and raising high the left one with the dark-amber bottle, he silently moved his lips, counting twelve, thirteen, four-teen and then very rapidly, as if running on tiptoe, fifteen-sixteenseventeen, and again slowly, to twenty. He wore a canary-yellow dressing gown; a pince-nez straddled the tip of his attentive nose.

And after another period of time, came spring, and a smell of mastic pervaded the staircase. In the house just across the street somebody died, and for quite a while there was a funereal automobile standing there, of a glossy black, like a grand piano. Graf was tormented by nightmares. He thought he saw tokens in everything, the merest coincidence frightened him. The folly of chance is the logic of fate. How not to believe in fate, in the infallibility of its promptings, in the obstinacy of its purpose, when its black lines persistently show through the handwriting of life?

The more one heeds coincidences the more often they happen. Graf reached a point when having thrown away the newspaper sheet out of which he, an amateur of mis-prints, had cut out the phrase "after a song and painful ill-ness," he saw a few days later that same sheet with its neat little window in the hands of a marketwoman who was wrapping up a head of cabbage for him; and the same evening, from beyond the remotest roofs a misty and malignant cloud began to swell, engulfing the first stars, and one suddenly felt such a suffocating heaviness as if carrying upstairs on one's back a huge iron-forged trunk—and presently, without warning, the sky lost its balance and the huge chest clattered down the steps. Graf hastened to close and curtain the casement, for as is well known, drafts and electric light attract thunderbolts. A flash shone through the blinds and to determine the distance of the lightning's fall he used the domestic method of counting: the thunder-clap came at the count of six which meant six versts. The storm increased. Dry thunderstorms are the worst. The windowpanes shook and rumbled. Graf went to bed, but then imagined so vividly the lightning's striking the roof any moment now, passing through all seven floors and transforming him on the way into a convulsively contracted Negro, that he jumped out of bed with a pounding heart (through the blind the casement flashed, the black cross of its sash cast a fleeting shadow upon the wall) and producing loud clanging sounds in the dark, he removed from the washstand and placed on the floor a heavy faïence basin (rigorously wiped) and stood in it, shivering, his bare toes squeaking against the earthenware, virtually all night, until dawn put a stop to the nonsense.

During that May thunderstorm Graf descended to the most humiliating depths of transcendental cowardice. In the morning a break occurred in his mood. He considered the merry bright-blue sky, the arborescent designs of dark humidity crossing the drying asphalt, and realized that only one more month remained till the nineteenth of June. On that day he would be thirty-four. Land! But would he be able to swim that distance? Could he hold out?

He hoped he could. Zestfully, he decided to take extraordinary measures to protect his life from the claims of fate. He stopped going out. He did not shave. He pretended to be ill; his landlady took care of his meals, and through her Mr. Engel would transmit to him an orange, a magazine, or laxative powder in a dainty little envelope. He smoked less and slept more. He worked out the crosswords in the émigré papers, breathed through his nose, and before going to bed was careful to spread a wet towel over his bedside rug in order to be at once awakened by its chill, if his body tried, in a somnambulistic trance, to sneak past the surveillance of thought.

Would he make it? June the first. June the second. June the third. On the tenth the neighbor inquired through the door if he was all right. The eleventh. The twelfth. The thirteenth. Like that world-famous Finnish runner who throws away, before the last lap, his nickel-plated watch which has helped him to compute his strong smooth course, so Graf, on seeing the end of the track, abruptly changed his mode of action. He shaved off his straw-colored beard, took a bath, and invited guests for the nineteenth.

He did not give in to the temptation of celebrating his birthday one day earlier, as slyly advised by the imps of the calendar (he was born in the previous century when there were twelve, not thirteen, days between the Old Style and the New, by which he lived now); but he did write to his mother in Pskov asking her to apprise him of the exact hour of his birth. Her reply, however, was rather evasive: "It happened at night. I remember being in great pain."

The nineteenth dawned. All morning, his neighbor could be heard walking up and down in his room, displaying unusual agitation, and even running out into the corridor whenever the front-door bell rang, as if he awaited some message. Graf did not invite him to the evening party— they hardly knew each other after all—but he did ask the landlady, for Graf's nature oddly united absentmindedness and calculation. In the late afternoon he went out, bought vodka, meat patties, smoked herring, black bread.... On his way home, as he was crossing the street, with the unruly provisions in his unsteady embrace, he noticed Mr. Engel illumined by the yellow sun, watching him from the balcony.

Around eight o'clock, at the very moment that Graf, after nicely laying the table, leaned out of the window, the following happened: at the corner of the street, where a small group of men had collected in front of the pub, loud angry cries rang out followed suddenly by the cracking of pistol shots. Graf had the impression that a stray bullet whistled past his face, almost smashing his glasses, and with an "akh" of terror, he drew back. From the hallway came the sound of the front-door bell. Trembling, Graf peeped out of his room, and simultaneously, Ivan Ivanovich Engel, in his canary-yellow dressing gown, swept into the hallway. It was a messenger with the telegram he had been awaiting all day. Engel opened it eagerly—and beamed with joy.

"Was dort für Skandale?" asked Graf, addressing the messenger, but the latter—baffled, no doubt, by his questioner's bad German—did not understand, and when Graf, very cautiously, looked out of the window again, the sidewalk in front of the pub was empty, the janitors sat on chairs near their porches, and a bare-calved housemaid was walking a pinkish toy poodle.

At about nine all the guests were there—three Russians and the German landlady. She brought five liqueur glasses and a cake of her own making. She was an ill-formed woman in a rustling violet dress, with prominent cheekbones, a freckled neck, and the wig of a comedy mother-in-law. Graf's gloomy friends, émigré men of letters, all of them elderly, ponderous people, with various ailments (the tale of which always comforted Graf), immediately got the landlady drunk, and got tight themselves without growing merrier. The conversation was, of course, conducted in Russian; the landlady did not understand a word of it, yet giggled, rolled in futile coquetry her poorly penciled eyes, and kept up a private soliloquy, but nobody listened to her. Graf every now and then consulted his wristwatch under the table, yearned for the nearest chuchtower to strike midnight, drank orange juice and took his pulse. By midnight the vodka gave out and the landlady, staggering and laughing her head off, fetched a bottle of cognac. "Well, your health, *staraya morda* (old fright)," one of the guests coldly addressed her, and she naively, trustfully, clinked glasses with him, and then stretched toward another drinker but he brushed her away.

At sunrise Grafitski said good-bye to his guests. On the little table in the hallway there lay, he noticed, now torn open and discarded, the telegram that had so delighted his neighbor. Graf abstractly read it: SOGLASEN PRODLENIE (extension agreed), then he returned to his room, introduced some order, and, yawning, replete with a strange sense of boredom (as if he had planned the length of his life according to the prediction, and now had to start its construction all over again) sat down in an armchair and flipped through a dilapidated book (somebody's birthday present)—a Russian anthology of good stories and puns, published in the Far East: "How's your son, the poet?"—"He's a sadist now"—"Meaning?" —"He writes only sad distichs." Gradually Graf dozed off in his chair and in his dream he saw Ivan Ivanovich Engel singing couplets in a garden of sorts and fanning his bright-yellow, curly-feathered wings, and when Graf woke up the lovely June sun was lighting little rainbows in the landlady's liqueur glasses, and everything was somehow soft and luminous and enigmatic—as if there was something he had not understood, not thought through to the end, and now it was already too late, another life had begun, the past had withered away, and death had quite, quite removed the meaningless memory, summoned by chance from the distant and humble home where it had been living out its obscure existence.